Golden Streak Series Book 5

KATHI S. BARTON

WCP

World Castle Publishing, LLC
Pensacola, Florida

Copyright © Kathi S. Barton 2014
Print ISBN: 9781629891484
eBook ISBN: 9781629891491
First Edition World Castle Publishing, LLC, September 5, 2014
http://www.worldcastlepublishing.com

Licensing Notes

Cover: Karen Fuller
Editor: Eric Johnston
Editor: Maxine Bringenberg

Chapter 1

"Bloody hell." Lenny looked at the rotation and cursed again. "This is not going to work and I fucking know it. Who comes up with this shit anyway?"

"I do." She turned to look at her captain, a big burly man called, of all things, Little Joe, although his name was Joseph Mason. "You have a problem with it, Red? If so, I don't really give a good flying fuck. I want you to shut the fuck up about it and get to work. Rice, your new partner, is waiting on you."

"Stop calling me fucking *Red*. It's Lenny, or if that doesn't suit, MacFinley. I'm in no mood for your jokes today. And he's a fucking rookie. I don't do rookies and you know it. They're…well hell, they're still suckling at their mom's tit, and I don't have time to wipe milk off their chins. I have a job to do."

"And today your job is wet nurse to Rice. Get the fuck out of here and get to that crime scene like you should have been ten minutes ago. What the fuck are you doing, having a fucking tea party? You know how I like punctuality." He'd stretched the word out to sound much longer than its five syllables. She wanted to punch him in the face.

Lenny took the keys off her desk and her gun out of her desk drawer and shoved it in her holster. She had no idea who this Rice character was, but he wasn't going to last the day with her. She'd make his life so miserable that he'd be begging for another partner. She was smiling as she went to pick up her car from the garage.

A man who she figured was David Rice was standing next to the car she'd been assigned to when she'd totaled the last one three weeks ago. Not that it had been her fault, but she had been in pursuit of a bank robber and he was getting away. It had taken her two weeks to get back out from behind the desk due to her injuries, and she wasn't going to end up there again because of some kid who was going to get in her way. And the closer she got to her new partner, the less she liked him.

"Wow, you sure are pretty." She stopped moving and glared at him. "I mean, I was told you were a looker, but I never thought they were so right."

He smiled at her and put out his hand. She ignored it and got in the car. He was still scrambling for his seat belt when she put the car in reverse and pulled out of the space. She glanced over at him when he held on to the "oh shit bar," the nice little extra her other partner had had put in to hang onto before he'd transferred out of homicide two days ago. Driving to her was like a sport. If she could make it through the day without killing or maiming someone, she gave herself a gold star. She was sure this wasn't going to be a gold-star day.

"What are we doing first?" She glanced over at him, wondering if he was serious. "I know we're going to a death, but what do—?"

"Okay, first and foremost, I am not pretty. You say that to me again and I will make a necklace out of your tongue and balls and make you wear it. Secondly, we're going to a homicide, not a death. A death is what you have at funeral homes. We're going to see who was murdered, figure out why some fuck did it, and arrest him. Thirdly, and this should have been first, the pretty comment pissed me off. But you don't talk unless I let you. Not a single word, not a grunt, and in no way are you to make any kind of hand signals." He actually raised his hand and she rolled her eyes. "What the fuck is that?"

"I'm asking for permission to speak." She looked at the road and counted to ten while he said whatever the fuck he wanted. "Do you want me to observe you and take notes? I want to learn from the best and I understand you're the best."

She didn't answer him. If she had to spend more than today with him, he wasn't going to live to collect his first paycheck and she'd be getting hers in prison. Taking the turn a little too fast, she skidded to a stop in front of the house where five people had allegedly been murdered. She got out and left him to either follow or stay. Right now she didn't care.

"Family of five, two adults and three kids dead, plus the dog. Looks like they killed him first…to shut him up, we're guessing. Neighbor said he was a barker, but last night he'd been quiet. Said he shut his yap around three. Vet is seeing if he can pinpoint a time for us." She nodded at the officer who'd met her at the door. She was pulling on her booties when Rice came racing up the walk.

"Who we got on site?"

Officer Beckley said, "The coroner and five assistants. I have six men working the streets."

"Where is the first victim? And make sure you let me know if the vet finds anything like how the barker was killed."

They were walking up the steps when Rice tapped her on the shoulder. "We use vets to give us time of death? Why not use the coroner? He's here. I saw his van out front."

She looked at him. "Are you related to the mayor? Or maybe the chief or someone high on the food chain? Gotta be something like that or you'd have never made it this far."

"My uncle is the mayor. How did you know?"

She didn't answer him but made a mental note to stop by the mayor's office and congratulate him on his DNA. The fucking prick had to have had sex with his sister to have a moron like this one.

It took her five hours to process the scene. It might have taken less time, but she was having too much fun with Rice now that she knew he had a weak stomach. Every time he entered a room after throwing up for a good ten minutes, she'd do something else to set him off. And a few of the officers who knew her well were joining in on the game. The last time Rice had taken off it was because Officer Beckley had gagged when he'd lifted the hand up that had been found under the bed. When he gagged loudly the second time Rice had paled so much that she wondered if he would ever recover. It had been the best scene she'd ever worked in terms of lessening the normal tension at a murder site.

Little Joe entered the last room she was processing just after sunset. He didn't look happy either. She finished what she was doing and sent the other officers out. If he was going to chew her ass off, she wanted him to do it in private. She wanted that like she did her praise, quiet and no fuss.

"There's been another killing. A family again." She looked around the room she was in and decided that murder and killing were not words she'd use to label what had been done here. This was a massacre. Whoever had done this had torn these people apart without any sort of method to his madness. Or so it seemed to her.

"Like this one?" He nodded. "How many? And please tell me that you're not going to make me take Rice with me. It's been fun and all, but he's not a homicide detective."

"No, he called me and said he was going home. I explained to him nicely that if he did, he wasn't coming back. Thanks for helping me out with that." She eyed him sharply. "Yeah, I knew you'd nip this shit in the bud. I don't need the mayor's nephew hanging around like it's halftime at one of his frat parties. Tell me what you have here and we'll compare notes."

"Five dead, looks like the woman was first. He got her in the kitchen. Her throat was ripped out and he gutted her. Then he took time to tie her up with them. Even arranged her hair with her blood. The next two were the kids, around eight and ten. The littler one was killed in the bathroom; same time was taken with her, but she'd had her head torn off, too. The older one was in the middle of the room. He had his throat cut and then was eviscerated as well, but left where he lay. I don't know why, but I think maybe the killer heard something and didn't finish. There was an infant in the crib of the parents' room and her neck was broken. Didn't do anything else but kill her. The father, however, he took his time with." They were going up the stairs and she pointed out the rooms where the others had been found. When they got to the master bedroom, he hesitated. "The baby's been taken out."

He nodded. She knew he couldn't handle the death of a child, and the younger the child, the worse it was for him. She waited until he gave her the okay before she moved in with him. Keeping his back to the crib, he listened attentively as she told him what she had found there.

"The male had been out of the bed when the first blow hit him. It looks like he had his arm out and when the blade sliced at him, he lost his hand. Then the second time he was hit, it looks like he fell to his knees and then to his belly. Whoever it was flipped him over and worked on him." The blood had shown that the man had tried to crawl away, but she didn't point that out. Mason was a good detective, too.

She looked at the sheet-covered male as she continued. "He didn't like this man, or maybe men in general. He wanted him last for a reason, and he showed me how much he really hated him. He cut off his dick, and then cut out his eyes while he was still alive. The removal of his tongue was probably all that kept him from waking the neighborhood. I think he would have bled out by the time he got to his balls and cut them off. Then he removed his fingers from his other hand and his toes before he tore out his heart. It's all right there."

"What do you mean?" She picked up a corner of the sheet to show him. "Holy mother of God, he arranged them."

He had, too. The parts that had been cut out were laying separate from the body, yet in the positions they might have been in prior to being removed. The fingers and toes were where arms and legs would have been, and his eyes and tongue were lying next to the head, all arranged together, as were his dick and balls at his groin area.

"I think he was trying to make a statement with art, but I can't think what it might be. He had hours to do this, too. I mean, just the woman downstairs would have taken time. But this...." She looked at the sheet that was bloodstained. "He would have had to work for several hours. More than the timeframe we have for the dog to stop barking and the call to come in. I don't think he was working alone."

"Two monsters like this?" She nodded. "Then we have the one across town. Christ, Red, this is not going to set well with the papers. And the mayor will have heard by now from the nephew. This is going to go down very badly with a great many people." They talked a little more about the art of the murders. There were no notes laying around, nothing to indicate that the house had been broken into either. Someone had let them in or they'd had a key. Either way, this wasn't a friend.

They were going down the hall when Mason turned to her. "You going over to the other site now? I have an officer there now waiting if you were going. The team is supposed to go after they clean up here."

"Yeah, no reason to wait." He grimaced at her and told her he guessed not. "You coming with me? I don't have a partner now and I suppose you'll do. Oh yeah, you pull that shit on me again and I'll quit."

"No you won't. You love this job too much to do that."

She rode over in his car, because, like most people who knew her, he was well aware of her driving habits.

She laughed at him when he stopped at a yellow light, and laughed harder when he used his turn signal.

"You're such a wuss. You should live a little. Sometime when you're driving use the opposite signal you need and turn. People just love it when you fuck with them." He glared and she laughed harder. "What do you know about this place?"

"Nothing. The officer on scene called it in to me when I was on my way over. He said that he would call the team in and have them get started." They pulled up in front of the house he'd pointed to. "I wonder where everyone is."

She felt the hair on the back of her neck dance. Something was off. The cruiser out front was running and the door open. She pulled her gun before releasing the seat belt. She heard Mason call in to someone, but she slipped out of the car and to the cruiser to see what might have happened. He was two steps behind her when she arrived at the car.

"Nothing here but his pad and his coat." She reached in and moved the coat carefully and didn't see anything. She looked at Mason. "Should we go in or — ?"

The scream had them both racing for the house. Mason tossed a vest at her and she was jerking it on while he was snapping his into place. By the time they got to the front door, a second and then a third scream came from deep inside. She looked at Mason and whispered.

"You or me?" He nodded that he'd take the lead. When he turned the handle on the door, she felt something rush over her, a feeling that they shouldn't go in, and turned to tell him that when he was suddenly not there.

Something had snatched him from the open doorway, and his gun and left shoe lay where he'd been standing.

She stared at them both before she reached down and picked up his Glock. Putting it into the back of her pants, she tried not to think about whom or what could have done what she was pretty sure she'd seen. Moving into the house, she saw the blood and leaned down to look. A slight breeze over her neck was the only warning she had.

The…creature had leapt over her, and she was sure had she not bent when she had he would have taken off her head. Lifting her gun, she fired four times and watched as each bullet entered his chest. When he floated up off the floor, she took off running to the door again.

"You'll never make it, my dear." As she touched the door she felt him cut her. He laughed and hit her again. This time instead of her arm, he hit her leg. He kept slicing at her over and over until she fell. She had no idea why she thought so, but he seemed to be toying with her. Firing at him again, she hit him in the head this time as well as the gut, and anywhere else she could until the slide snapped back that it was empty.

She looked down at her body and saw that she was losing blood fast. He'd cut her over a dozen times, and she knew that his next cut was going to end her. When she looked up the stairs, she saw the second creature, and he was…he had his mouth over Mason's throat, and when he lifted his head, blood dripped off his chin onto his snowy white shirt. Mason was dead; even from where she lay she could see that. The one nearest her moved close enough that she could feel his hot, rancid breath on her face.

"Do you like what you see there? Would you like to join your fat friend in the afterlife? I'll be more than glad to take you. I know that we're only to kill you, but to have you with me for all time would be more than the payment we're supposed to receive to do this for her. It would be so cool to have her pissed off for a while just to fuck you even for one night." She shook her head, dizzy now and fading quicker. He lifted his hand up so she could see it and she watched in horror as it morphed into a claw with sharp talons. He pressed it into her vest and through it. As it pierced her chest, she felt something under her hand. Lifting it up, she nearly dropped it twice before she could see what it was…a sliver of wood.

He growled low, and she felt from his closeness that he was upset, angry with her. She figured he was pissed because she was more willing to die than spend time with him. "Then I suppose you shall have to die." She was doing that already, but she took the wood shard and, using the last of her strength, rammed it into his face. As she was dying, she heard his screams and smiled.

"Shouldn't talk when you're killing someone. Bad plot line." Laughing at her own stupid joke, she felt blood spill from her mouth. "Christ, Mason, we should have waited for backup."

She must have blurred out for several seconds, she figured. Hell, it could have been an hour, but she didn't think so. She was bleeding to death, and it wouldn't take an hour, not with all the blood she'd already lost. A man suddenly appeared in front of her, and she tried to back away.

"I'll not hurt you." She felt his touch and wondered why it felt so warm. "You are going to die, my child."

"No fucking shit, moron." She coughed again and more blood splattered over her shirt. "Can you help Mason?"

"I am afraid I cannot. He was gone before I arrived." He pressed something to her mouth, and she tried to pull away. "Just a sip to get you to the hospital. Then you will be in their hands."

"Not going to make it to hospital." She wasn't stupid. "Dead. Tell Grandma that I'm sorry for all…every…."

Her body was so cold, and she closed her eyes. A coppery taste seemed to spread over her tongue, but she didn't care. Her own blood was dripping off her in buckets; some of it was bound to get into her mouth. She looked up again when someone said her name, and she tried to focus.

"Are you listening, my child?" She tried to speak but nothing was working. "You must hang on for a few moments more. He will need you to save him and the others."

She was dreaming. She'd read about it, people having these sorts of dreams as they died. She had no doubt that she was dying either; she'd been cut to hell and nothing was going to save her. She closed her eyes again and felt her breath leave her body. "I'm sorry."

~~~

Peter held her hand and willed her to live. He'd been too late to keep her from going into this house, but he had to save her now. Her partner was gone, as he'd told her, but he'd been changed as well. Peter had taken care that he would not rise, but the man was still dead.

Peter looked at the ash around her. She'd killed one of them while she lay there bleeding. He had to smile at that. She was going to make a good warrior for the Golden family…if she lived. She had refused his blood and he'd had to use other means to give her a fighting chance.

"She will not die." He looked up at the man who was his master. "She is stronger than you think. Much stronger than any of us think. She will need to be."

"If she dies today, it is because of me." Viktor shook his head. "I should have known that they would come for her. I should have been watching her closer when I woke them. It was my plan to have them weak with need when they all arrived, but feeding on the partner helped them harm her. And I should have also known that she would go into this house before backup arrived. She is most stubborn."

"That she is. But you did what you could. And she would have come no matter how hard you would have tried to stop her. She is very…strong. She will be of a great help to the others." Peter nodded and thought, *Only if she lives*. "I can give her more of my blood if it will make you believe me."

She'd refused Peter's so he couldn't give it to her even if she was unconscious. But she hadn't been able to refuse his master, and he'd fed her only a few drops of his own blood. It was stronger than Peter's, but they could not give her too much, for if she was healed completely, it would cause her more problems.

When he heard the sirens, he faded out but didn't leave her. She was breathing now, but it was shallow and her heart was beating entirely too slowly for his peace of mind. When the first officer entered the house, he nearly tripped over her, and would have had Peter not kept him from falling. He would have killed her if he had. He called in "officer down" immediately and help was on the way.

"She will make it now." Peter nodded at Viktor as they both hovered above the scene. "She has killed one. That will leave only five to go. The one that escaped here and the other group that still lays in waiting."

"I have tried to find them, but they are hidden well. But they have formed a nest. They reside somewhere in

New York. But I fear after this they will move to where she is going. Things are not going to be easy for her and her mate." He looked at Viktor. "How did they know about her so quickly? Is it her sire?"

Viktor told him he didn't know. They both moved closer as the medics arrived. They were working very hard to save her, but she lost the battle. Peter touched her head with his magic and she took another breath. The team doubled their efforts, and with the help of Viktor, she was loaded into the waiting ambulance.

"Her death would change things." Peter nodded, not knowing what it would change but knowing that her survival was going to be important to a great many people, them included. "She will be different, stronger than before."

"She will need it, I think. Should we take her memories from her of us?" Viktor said he thought she should have them but to fade them for a time. Peter agreed and put the encounter with them in the back of her mind to pull up later.

"We will need to prepare things with the Golden artist. He will need to know that she comes." Peter shook his head. "You think to surprise him with her? He will not like that, I think."

"He'll love her and that's all that matters. If we need to tell him, I will, but I have found that humans and shifters alike enjoy the chase of their mates. Jules will not want a mate like her, and it would go better for them both if they find each other without our help. For a time anyway."

They stayed with Lenny until she was stable. She could still die, they knew, but at this point couldn't interfere again without repercussions that would harm the girl. Peter went to the hospital to keep her safe, he told himself, but he knew it was only to make sure. She would live, she was needed, but her death needed to be monitored to see what effects it might have had when Viktor brought her back. He could only hope that she didn't have anything that would terrify her. Although he'd seen her drive and doubted much terrified the young human, he knew that there were some things that could even frighten him, and he'd seen a great deal in his lifetime.

Chapter 2

(Eight weeks later)

"I'm just going to stay until I can make it on my own." Lenny's grandma nodded. "The doctors don't want me staying by myself until I get stronger. I won't be a bother."

Lenny looked away when she saw the tears on her grandma's face. She'd been doing that since she'd picked her up last night and all the way on the plane to Ohio. It hurt her to see such a strong woman cry, and she didn't know what to do.

"You say you're a bother to me once more and I'll make you walk the rest of the way home." Lenny smiled. It was the same threat she'd used on her when she'd been a child. "You're staying with me until you're perfectly healed. Then I'm kicking you to the curb. Understand me?"

"Yes, ma'am." Lenny shifted on the seat and tried not to moan. The ride to the airport hadn't been too bad, but the car was too small for her to stretch out in and her leg was throbbing again. But she was out of the hospital and away from all the newspaper people and the cops...the cops especially.

She'd not told anyone what had happened. None of it. She knew that something more than just humans had been in that house, and that they'd killed her and her boss. Lenny had been told several times that she'd been resuscitated three times before she was brought in. She also knew that a man had been there after she'd stabbed the killer, but she hadn't told anyone that either. Actually, she wasn't sure what to tell them, especially about the man she'd killed.

A thing had grabbed Mason so fast his shoe had come off and he'd dropped his gun. Whatever it was had tried to take off her head and had sliced her up with nothing more than his hands. And at one point another one like him had bitten into Mason and drank his blood. Yeah, that would go over really well around the big house. She looked out the window and tried to think of anything else but the pain.

"I have your prescription if you need something." Lenny shook her head. "I can stop and get you something to eat if you need to take it with food."

"I do, but I'm hurting too bad to eat right now, and if I take the meds this close to home, you'll have to leave me in the car because you won't be able to carry me inside. I'll be fine until we get there." She tried to smile at her but it hurt too much. "Thank you for letting me stay with you. I know that we didn't part on very good—"

"We're both too stubborn to not fight. You're too much like me. I thought that was a good thing and now…they said you should have been…they didn't know how you lived as long as you did. I told them you were a MacFinley and you didn't know the word quit."

Grandma was right on that. Lenny should have died and stayed dead. She glanced at the woman she'd once thought of as her grandma and thought about the day she'd left, swearing to never return. Had it only been eight years ago? Lenny had been seventeen and her head full of shit.

The woman who'd been her grandma, Nicee MacFinley, had been caring for her since she'd been born. Lenny's mother had dropped her off with her one day, she'd been told, and simply never returned. Lenny had always thought that her parents had found another daughter who didn't embarrass them as much as Lenny had, but on the day she left, her grandmother had told her the truth.

~~~

"They're in prison, both of them. And have been since the day you moved in here."

Lenny had stared at her grandma for several seconds, not understanding or maybe not wanting to. "Why?" Grandma started to tell her what they had done, but Lenny shook her head. "Why did you lie to me? I don't care what they did, but you lied to me."

"It was for the best. I didn't think you knowing would help you in life, so I told you that so you'd think they might come back for you. I didn't want you to know what horrible people they were." At that time she had no idea how right her grandma was in calling them horrible. All she could think about was that she'd been lied to. "If you had known, you would have told someone and others would have found out. I did it to protect you."

"You can't protect someone from the truth. You can't stand there and tell me you did this all for me. You just didn't want your garden club to find out. You didn't want to lose face." Her grandma hadn't denied it, and Lenny took that to mean it was the truth and had left without a backward glance.

~~~

"They're...my father is dead. I did some investigating and found out." She glanced at her grandma when she heard the sharp intake of breath. "And they weren't in a regular prison, as you know, so they don't have the sort of records that are easy to get to or hack into."

"So you were able to find out about them then?" Lenny knew that her grandma had never liked her parents for some reason. She didn't know her whole story yet, but hoped with this visit she'd get some answers. *Hell of a way to find out*, she thought.

"I know who they were and that they weren't human. My mother was supposed to be a vampire, and my father...I don't know what. There was some confusion as to what he was, and it's doubtful that he told the truth concerning it either."

Her grandmother didn't say anything, but Lenny could see the relief on her face. Her parents were not nice people, and their record, what she was able to find out about it, wasn't anything that surprised her so much as it made her raise a brow. Why weren't these people dead by the hand of the law? Even after she'd left home, Lenny had made no effort to see them, not after she'd looked them up.

The house came into view a few minutes later. It was the same, but someone had given it a new paint job. There were bigger bushes out front and the lawn needed to be mowed, too, but it looked the same.

When the car stopped, Lenny waited until her grandma came around to help her. Lenny had promised the doc if he let her go early, she'd be extra careful and learn to ask for help instead of thinking she was invincible. She knew she wasn't, but the man had a point about asking for help.

She was sweating by the time she made it to the little room that had been set up for her. The bedrooms were on the second and third floor and she would never have made it up the stairs. The insurance she had through the police had provided her with the equipment she needed to use…a bed and all the exercise equipment she would need to regain her strength. She was set for life, it seemed.

After her grandma brought her some soup and a glass of water, Lenny took a pill and let the pain meds take her away. She was feeling the effects of them when her grandma came back in the room to take the tray.

"I have a friend coming over to help me give you a bath." Lenny could only nod. "She's a real sweetheart, and you'll probably hate her on sight."

"Will not. Sooner." Her grandma laughed. Lenny smiled and closed her eyes. She hoped that whoever this person was had a strong stomach. Even she had a hard time looking at the destruction done to her body by that monster.

~~~

Bronwyn pulled into Mrs. MacFinley's driveway at six-thirty. She'd meant to be there sooner, but Gabby had taken her first steps, and she'd been so excited that she'd called everyone and had forgotten about the time. She went to the back of her car, pulled her daughter out of the car seat, and took her up to the big house. When the door opened, she smiled at the elderly woman.

"I'm so sorry I'm late. Gabby walked from the desk to the couch and I simply forgot the time." Grandma shushed her and took the baby. "I think she likes you more than me sometimes."

"It's because I give her cookies." Nicee, as she had insisted she call her, snuggled Gabby to her body and kissed her. "Come in, come in. Lenny is still asleep, but she wanted me to wake her soon. She had to take a full dose of medicine and I think it put her out."

Bronwyn had read what had happened to the young woman from a report that Brock had had done when she'd said she was going to help out some. Bronwyn didn't know the younger woman, of course, but she was sure that the papers she'd read were guessing on what had happened to her and didn't know the actual truth, whatever that had been. The investigator had said that the young detective couldn't remember much other than pulling up to the house. Bronwyn wondered if that was true. It had apparently been very horrific, so much so that Nicee could hardly talk about what had been done to her granddaughter.

"I'll just go and check on her." Bronwyn stood up and said she'd go, but Nicee warned her first. "She's a tad on the…she's never been one to hold her tongue. You should let me go and wake her, and warn her as to what's going on."

"I have five brothers-in-law, Nicee. Whatever Lenny says to me, I'm sure it won't hurt my feelings." She moved to what would have been the parlor when the house was built and knocked on the door. The crash on the other side made her open the door quickly.

"Get the fuck out of here." Bronwyn ignored her and went to the bed to help. "I've fucking got it. Christ. I'm sick."

Bronwyn handed her the trash can, which she guessed the girl had been going after. As soon as she put it up to her face, Bronwyn could hear her retching hard. Bronwyn straightened up the room while Lenny rested.

"Feel better?" The girl glared at her. "Let me help you get those clothes off. You've gotten them covered."

"Get out. I can do it myself." Bronwyn took the can from her, set it by the door, and came back. "Are you listening to me? I said to get out."

"Oh, I heard you all right, but I'm here to help give you a bath, so we do this my way or the hard way. Either way, you're not going to lay there in your own puke." Bronwyn reached for the buttons and Lenny grabbed her. For someone as pale as she was, she was incredibly strong.

"I…I'm a mess." Bronwyn nodded. "No, I mean they sort of had to slap me back together, and I'm a mess. I can do this. I can't…the trash can is full and you might need it."

"How bad is it?" Lenny looked away but didn't let go of the shirt. "Lenny, let me help you. You can't do this on your own. Please?"

"Don't say I didn't warn you."

Bronwyn's heart went out to the woman. She opened all the buttons but didn't open her shirt yet. She looked up at her. This was not the victim of a heart attack and a fall as she knew the grandmother had been told.

"Should I get your grandmother?" Lenny shook her head. "Has she seen you yet? Seen what happened to you."

"No. I won't…I won't do that to her after what I've done to her before. She's…she's all I have left."

Bronwyn nodded and pulled open her shirt. Peeling back the bloodied gauze, she could see why the girl had warned her.

Claw marks. They went from one side of her belly to the other. Long, pink, and ugly scars as wide as an inch marred her pale skin. There were dark stitches still in some areas, while staples were along the rest of them. Bronwyn wondered if Lenny should be there or at the hospital still.

"I couldn't stay any longer. I was…it was too hard on me there with all the press and police wanting to know what I remembered or knew. And then Mason's daughter showed up, wanting answers. I couldn't tell her anything and she cried, begged for me to give her a reason why someone would cut off her dad's fucking head." She turned to look at her, and Bronwyn was shocked at the hatred she saw there. "Could you tell a kid that the reason someone cut off his head was because a fucking vampire was drinking from him? Can you imagine how well that would have gone over with the brass? But that's what I fucking remember…a man drinking from my friend and blood dripping from his mouth, all while another one played with me and sliced me to shit with his claws."

"No." Lenny turned away from her as she continued. "No, I wouldn't be able to either. I think you moving here with your grandmother is the best move."

Lenny helped her as best she could as she got out of the bed. The linens needed to be changed, and giving her a bath proved to be exhausting enough as it was without trying to do it in a hospital bed. Just as she was helping Lenny pull on another set of clothes, these made of soft terry, her grandmother came in with Gabby.

Gabby usually didn't take well to strangers. It had taken her nearly two months to let Nicee hold her without crying. Now she loved the woman. But she crawled right to the chair that Lenny was sitting in and pulled herself up to see her. Before Nicee could go and pull her away, Bronwyn's daughter tried to crawl up in Lenny's lap.

"Hey, kid, I'm not much of a baby person." Gabby laughed, and Lenny smiled at her. "So you're a charmer, are you? You must get that from your dad. Your mom is a pain in the as…butt."

"She does take after her father a great deal." Bronwyn tucked the sheet into the mattress and went to pick up her little girl. "I'll hold her. She just wants to say hi to you."

"Sit her here, please." Lenny pointed to her right thigh. Bronwyn hadn't seen her body from the waist down because she wouldn't allow it, but she'd bet anything that she was no less scarred there. When she sat Gabby on her thigh, Lenny winced but didn't ask to have her moved. Bronwyn sat close enough to get her if need be.

"My friend had two little girls. One was eight; the other was twelve. He loved them very much." Lenny touched Gabby's dark hair. "He couldn't stand to see little kids hurt."

"The paper said you claimed to have been on a call that had —" Bronwyn closed her mouth when Lenny shook her head. "I'm sorry."

"He was with me in the house. He…he died." Lenny let Gabby pull on her hair, and when she started to crawl closer, Bronwyn had to take her, as Lenny looked to be in a great deal of pain. "I'm not well enough for her energy yet."

Nicee and Bronwyn finished up the room and left Lenny where she was. She'd fallen back to sleep and they both thought she needed it. When they were sitting in the kitchen having a cup of tea, Nicee looked at her.

"She's hurt badly, isn't she?" Bronwyn nodded. "I thought so. When I went to the door to help you, I heard her say that she didn't want me to see. I could...I was going to say that I could handle it, but I don't think I can. I thank you for what you did today, but I should get a nurse. Lenny may let her help more."

"Should she be home yet?" Nicee shook her head. "I didn't think so. She looks like she needs more care than either of us can give her. I know a nurse. She's very dedicated and is looking for work right now. She works for us part time, but she's just bought a house and needs to have a little more income."

None of which was true, but she liked this woman and the one in the other room. There was something very...special about them.

Nicee stood up and refreshed their tea. "I don't have a great deal of money. I know that Lenny has insurance, but they will only cover so much. That's why I thought that I could do it, save us both some money." Nicee wiped at her cheeks, and Bronwyn's heart went out to her. "How much do you think she'd charge? I know when I looked into a service, they wanted well over what I get in Social Security every month. And Lenny's insurance only pays eighty dollars a day. Can you ask her for me?"

"I will." Bronwyn looked around the room as she sipped her tea. The room was spotless, but the place had a very worn...used looked to it. She'd had Neal look into the finances of the two of them, and neither of them lived above their means.

Lenny had gone to college by waiting tables and taking on odd jobs at the university that helped round out her grants…and had graduated in the top one percent of her class. Nicee had some money saved, but very little, and her pension was barely enough to keep her in food, much less meds, if her granddaughter needed anything more than she was currently taking for pain, which had been covered.

"When Lenny was seventeen, she wanted to go to a grand college. I didn't have the funding for that sort of thing, and I'd…I had lied to her about her parents. When she asked me if there was any way to contact them to help her, I had to tell her where they were. She didn't take it well." Bronwyn knew they'd been in prison but said nothing as Nicee continued. "She didn't take it well is an understatement, I guess. She left here and never returned. Not in all these years, but she sent me money every month. I couldn't have…I would have been homeless had she not helped me."

"She's a detective in Washington." Nicee shook her head, and Bronwyn tried to remember what Neal had told her. "I'm sorry, I thought I'd heard that—"

"She can't ever work again. They said she'd had a heart attack. That's what they told me anyway. I didn't believe it, of course, not the way they had her all bandaged up like they did. They told me that she'd fallen. Bullshit. She was hurt, but…." Nicee took a deep breath. "They lied to me. Something happened to her and now they want to blame her. When I went to get her on that fancy plane they sent me there to get her in, that man said that she was not to leave my house without their permission. If she had fallen like they said, what does her being tied to my house have to do with a simple fall?"

Bronwyn didn't know, but she planned to get to the bottom of it. When Neal, then Keith, had done a search, they both had said there was something off about the articles in the paper, but had told her that they were going to dig. Later, Keith told her that Lenny had been injured on the job, but he'd never told her how and she'd not inquired. Now she would.

On her way home she called Keith first. He told her that he'd been blocked out of the records, but if she would promise to help him out of jail if it went that far, he'd look. She promised him that she'd make sure he was never caught. Then she called Peter.

"I need you to do something for me." He told her anything she needed. "A friend of mine has a granddaughter that has been injured on the job. The place where she worked told her grandmother that she'd had a heart attack and fell down a flight of stairs. But today when I spoke to the girl, she said her friend had been bitten by a vampire, and the marks on her body do not look like they came from a fall."

"Lenore is here? She was supposed to be in the hospital for another month. Will that child ever do anything on a time table I can follow?" Bronwyn knew the exact moment that Peter realized he'd said too much. "Is she going to be okay? Did you read her mind?"

"No. I thought of it, but...I was afraid. I'm sure that whatever happened to her was horrific, and I just didn't want to know today. As for her being all right? I don't know. She's been hurt badly, there's no money for help, and she's being blamed for whatever happened to her and her friend. I'm assuming you know what happened to her, the real reason she looks like someone clawed her belly open." He told her he did. "And the reason you know this is why?"

"I was…." He took a deep breath. "I will pay for her care, but her grandmother, as well as Lenore, is very prideful, so if you could pave the way for me I'd—"

"I'm going to see if Sindy can care for her. She can get good care and I'll pay the difference. You want any information on the girl, you'll tell me what happened to her and why you know her."

"I can only tell you so much. But she was injured by the rogues that Brock and Em are helping the Realm with. She's…the rogue knew that she was important to me and wanted to kill her."

She pulled into her drive and looked at her daughter while she slept as she spoke to Peter. "Who is she to us? I know you well enough to know that you never do anything without a reason, so who is she to us?"

"She is Jules's mate."

Chapter 3

Jules watched the clay form. He loved this part of what he did, when he took a ball of fresh clay and put it onto the wheel and let it speak to him. Nothing in this whole process made him more pleased with what he did than this part. Second was taking the finished piece out of the kiln and seeing all the hard work come down to the finished product. He didn't look up when he felt someone come into his workshop, but let the piece continue. He knew it was his brother Ryland, but didn't care to speak to him just now, if ever again.

"Are you still pissed at me?" Jules took his hands off the piece as he let the anger toward Ryland move away. "I'm not leaving until we fix this."

"I'm trying to work. You want to talk, come back later. Right now I have eight more pieces to throw, and if you keep digging at me, I'll never get them done." He heard his brother mumble something about artists and their temperament, and had to take several deep breaths before he could put his hands on the piece. It took him several minutes of simply letting the piece turn on the wheel before he touched it again.

Lost in the work, he let the music of it roll over him. The workshop was silent now that everyone had gone for the day, but Jules had been listening to the clay for so long that he thought of it as music. When the first three pieces of the ten he would throw were sitting on the rack, he backed from his wheel and went to the sink. He'd hoped that Ryland had gotten tired of waiting and left, but that would just be too much to hope for. He was sitting at Jules's front desk playing on the computer when he walked in.

"Are you apologizing to me? If not, then get the fuck out of here." Ryland stood up and looked ready to do battle. "I'm dead serious, Ryland, say you're sorry or get out."

"The house was not what you—" Jules walked away. "Damn it, Jules. The house was not worth what they were asking for it. If I had paid what they were demanding, you would never have gotten your investment back even if you owned it for the next nine hundred years."

"I don't fucking care, you pigheaded louse. You knew I wanted that house. I've been telling you that for fifteen years. I said to you 'if the house comes on the market, buy it, and I'll pay you back.' How many times did I say that to you? A thousand, a million times in all these years?"

"He wanted just under a million dollars." That stopped Jules and he turned to his brother. "He had heard that we wanted it and he wouldn't budge on the price. The house appraised at less than half that just last year, and I couldn't get him to come down. The man who bought it said that he was going to resell it when he got it fixed up. There would be no amount of fixing that house that would give anyone a good return."

Jules started to ask if he'd told the new owner, but he knew Ryland better than that. He would do what it took to get something as cheaply as he could to make a profit.

There was no way there would be any profit in that house, not for a million dollars.

"Who bought it?" He told him the name of the man who had less sense than he did money. "Do you think he'll tear it down?"

"No. He borrowed the money to buy it and they won't let him. The good news is that he may have to sell it in a few years when the cost of repairing it outweighs what he has in it. You might be able to get it then." Ryland handed him a file. "The plumbing is shot to hell, the slate roof needs to be replaced, and most of the support-and load-bearing walls need to be either replaced or reinforced before you can do anything to the walls. The furnace is as old as I am, and there—" Jules cut him off. "It was going to be a bad investment no matter what you paid for it. I'm sorry."

"You could have told me this first thing yesterday." Ryland only smiled. "But then you wouldn't get to fight with me. You are the most pigheaded man I know. But I think I will have to let you slide on this one. For now."

"Not all bad, I suppose. You're pretty strong for someone that plays in the dirt all day." Ryland laughed. "Did I throw you off so badly that you can't do that thing for Bronwyn tomorrow?"

He'd forgotten about whatever it was he was doing. He had an alarm on his phone for it and something on his calendars at his apartment, but he couldn't remember what he was supposed to do. He looked at Ryland for help.

"You're taking that friend of hers to the doctor's office. Her relative can't help her in and out of their car very well."

He remembered now. Something about her being banged up pretty badly. "I'll be there. I have to be there at seven for an eight o'clock appointment, and I'm taking Bronwyn's car. She said it would be easier on her. I heard that Sindy is going to work for the girl, too." He hadn't heard what had happened to the child, only that she had been hurt pretty badly.

After Ryland left, he sat at his wheel again. The last of the pieces were easy after he and his brother had talked. He was still upset about the house but not with Ryland. Who would pay that much for a house that wasn't worth it? When he cleaned up his area and covered the wet pieces, he locked the door and went to his car.

There were four messages on his phone. One from Bronwyn reminding him to pick up Lenny tomorrow—for some reason Jules had thought the kid was a girl, and made a mental note to remember that tomorrow— and the last three were from his publicist. She needed an updated picture of him, a bio for the new catalog, as well as the piece he was going to put on the cover. He fixed a can of soup and ignored the messages. After his dinner he went to his computer and found the same messages, in email form, there as well. Closing it down, he went to the living room and sat in front of the television until he'd fallen asleep a half dozen times, then went to bed. Tomorrow was going to be a big day and he decided that when he was finished with this thing with the kid, he was going to go to the grocery store, then get to work. Things were not going to get done on their own.

At six forty-five he was at the house. He fell in love with it immediately and walked around the yard to get a better view from all angles twice before going to the door. Christ, this was just what he was looking for, and he wondered if the woman that owned it would think of selling. When an older woman answered, he was at a loss for words for several seconds. She had blood all over her shirt.

"Are you hurt?" She shook her head, but she was upset. "Where is the kid? Tell me where he is."

"I was helping with...Lenny is so much heavier than I thought, and when...." He put his hands on her shoulders to calm her down. "She's in there. But be careful. We dropped a glass and a tray of food."

He nodded and wondered who the "she" was and where the boy was. The room, when he entered, looked like a hospital room, complete with the bed and IV poles hanging from it. There was no one in the room, and he started to turn when he heard something. Going to the other side of the bed, he found a woman on the floor who was bleeding pretty heavily.

"I'm all right, Grandma. I just...just let me lay here until the pain meds kick in and I'll get up." She looked at him and Jules felt his world rock when he looked at the most gorgeous woman he'd ever seen. "Who the fuck are you?"

"Jules Golden. I'm here to take someone to the doctor's office. I'm assuming that would be you." He walked to the bleeding woman and started to reach for her. "How should I pick you up?"

"You fucking touch me and I'll kill you." He took a step back. Christ, she was pissed. "I'm sorry, but if you touch me it's only going to hurt more. And at the moment all I want to do is slip away on the nice drugs. Just let me lay here."

The blood had saturated her blouse, and he could see where her leg was bleeding, too. He thought she needed an ambulance, but before he could say anything he heard a siren. He looked at the doorway when who he now assumed was Mrs. MacFinley walked in.

"I've called them, honey." She was crying and he wanted to comfort the older woman. "I'm so sorry, baby. I didn't mean to drop you."

"I'm fine, Grandma. It's only a few stitches and I'll be as good as new once these guys put them back." Jules didn't think that was all it was going to take, but said nothing. The girl looked like she'd kick his ass even as hurt as she was if he dared to say a word. He smiled at her instead.

The medics came in and pulled her shirt up. It took them three tries to get Lenny to let it go, but when she did, his breath caught. Christ, she'd been more than banged up. The medic that was leaning over her froze when he cut away her pants.

"Get him out of here." He shook his head at her. "I said to leave. I don't need a fucking audience in here. Just go…away."

He didn't move, not even when the medic told him to. He did pull out his cell phone and call Bronwyn, after they'd given Lenny something else for the pain and she was out. They were loading her onto a gurney when Bronwyn answered. He was just telling them to take her to the Clinic, a medical facility that his family owned and operated.

"She's fallen." He heard her cuss. "And no, I didn't do it. She told the medics that she was getting up to go to the bathroom with her grandma's help and tripped up over something. Apparently her grandma had tried to hold her weight but they both tumbled. I think she took the brunt of the fall."

"I heard you tell them to take them to the Clinic. Good. Are you riding in with her or bringing her grandma?" He hadn't planned on either but thought it was a good idea. There was something about the girl—woman, he guessed—that made him think she needed protection, though he doubted he could take care of her any better than she could. She looked like she was as tough as nails, as his mom said.

"I'll be there, but I don't know which way yet. Are you going to meet us there?" She told him she would. "What the hell happened to her, Bronwyn? She's been sliced open all over her body."

"I don't know. Alistair is looking into some things for me, but all I can find out from anyone is that she'd fallen down a flight of stairs after suffering a heart attack." He snorted. "How much of her wounds did you see?"

"She's been clawed by a big animal, and he did a great deal of damage to her. Her belly, as well as her chest, is riddled with open wounds, and her legs are just as bad front and back. There is a mark on her chest that looks like someone tried to dig her heart out. And as for a heart attack? There is no way she got hurt like this from a fall, no matter what they say happened to her heart. Something or someone pierced her chest, and I'd bet my next check it was the same kind of claws that cut her up."

He told her they were on their way and he ended up following the ambulance with Nicee, as she'd asked him to call her, riding with him. She looked so distraught that he was worried for her as well. When he asked her what happened, she told the same story as Lenny had told the medics, but not quite the same.

"She needed to use the bathroom and I was helping her. But I had a little spell. I get all weak at times and I couldn't hold her. When she reached for the bed, it was too far away and the tray for her breakfast hit the floor and she tripped up in the tea. It was entirely my fault." When she burst into tears, Jules felt helpless. He handed her a box of tissues that were in the console and let her try to compose herself. When they pulled into the clinic, Lenny was already inside and the ambulance was parked in one of the reserved spaces. He pulled in right next to it.

~~~

Lenny was in so much pain it was all she could do not to scream every time someone touched her. And they touched her a lot. The nurse who had met her at the front doors had taken one look at her, rushed inside, and come back out with about a dozen people. Lenny was also getting sick. The pain medication didn't agree with her.

"Sick," she said to one of the nurses as he flew by her with some sort of instrument. And he gave her a little half-moon of a pan. "I need big."

When he only shoved it at her again, she knew it wasn't going to cut it, but it was too late now. As soon as she put it to her mouth, she screamed out her vomit. The pain was nearly unbearable and she was only getting sicker from it. Then the man from the house was standing there, barking at someone to help her.

Warmth ran along her arm where the medics had put in the IV, and she looked to see that someone was putting something in it. Before she could ask them what it was, she felt her head lull back and her neck get very soft. The man pulled her head around to look at him and she heard him saying something, but she couldn't hear it over her screams. She tried to close her mouth over them but the shakes started up, and she was fading fast.

"I hurt." He nodded and she felt a warmed blanket being put over her. "Hurt so bad. Should die."

"I don't think so. You'll have to live so I can claim you." That made no sense to her, so she closed her eyes. When he said her name, she looked up at him. "Who hurt you?"

"A vampire. I wish I had just died." The blackness came up to slap the shit out of her, and she let it. As she tumbled down the dark hole, she felt the pain recede and then felt herself smile. This was the good stuff she'd gotten in the hospital, not the generic stuff she could afford.

~~~

Peter watched her sleep. The damned girl was going to get herself killed if she didn't stay put. He smiled when he thought of what Jules had said to him an hour into her surgery. The man had figured out she was his mate.

"You'll tell me who did this to her. And I don't want any bullshit about how you can't do it, either. I want his name." He told him he was dead. "When? And if you tell me you did it, I'm going to kick your ass on principle."

"Lenore killed him when he hurt her. She was dying and picked up a sliver of wood and rammed it into his body, and he died instantly."

Jules only nodded and looked at him again. "Were you there? Did you see him hurt her?" Peter shook his head. "She...did you see what he did to her? How badly she's hurt? Someone fucking tried to strip her body apart one inch at a time. Why isn't she still in a hospital somewhere being treated with the proper medications?"

Peter told him he'd have to ask her that, and Jules finally walked away. That had been over six hours ago. And now she lay in recovery, after a surgery that had repaired what had torn open when she'd fallen. Peter looked up when Jules walked in.

"I've talked to her grandmother. She doesn't know anything, does she?" Peter told him that the police had lied to her about the injuries and other things. "I think you've already guessed it, but she's my mate. I have to help her."

"I understand. But she isn't going to be easy to convince of that. I believe that she has a way about her that will try and keep you away from her."

Jules laughed and told him he'd already figured that out. "She was cussing up a blue streak when I entered the room where they had her before surgery. One of the nurses asked her to stop cursing at her, and she threw back her sheet and the nurse stumbled back. I guess after that they figured she could scream all she wanted."

"She died while we waited for the first officer to come on scene. She had taken her last breath, and Viktor brought her back. We will not be able to help her that way again." Jules nodded. "She will live or die of her own accord now if she chooses."

Jules watched her, too, as the nurse came in and checked on her. They wouldn't be thrown out, and if the staff tried, he doubted either of them would leave. The Goldens ran and funded this facility. Peter would stay even if he had to do it so no one could see him. Jules asked him about her injuries.

"Her belly was ripped open, as were her arms and legs. He toyed with her for a while, I think, and she fought him back. I think she might have hurt him several times before he finally leaned over her to kill her. She would not give up. It's not in her nature." Peter stood up to look out the window. "They are saying that she is responsible for the death of the other officer, her superior. They are saying that she was lead on the case and she should have waited for backup. Then when she had her heart attack and fell, there could have been more personnel there to help and not leave the other officer to be killed. I've heard that she is considered somewhat of a hot-head and thinks herself above such petty things as laws. They have no record of the call coming in about where the two of them were, and nothing on any deaths at the scene that she was working prior to her getting hurt...no one knows what they were doing during that time."

"They were working another case? And no one was with them?" Peter didn't answer. "What do you think is going on, Peter? Something isn't right and we both know it."

"The other case involved the death of five people, a family. I have...I have taken the liberty of reading her mind, and there were several people there with her when she worked the crime scene. Most of them that were there have no recollection of any scene and have no memory of seeing her at all that day. The others, the ones that were closest to her, are dead as well." Peter looked back at the bed. "Someone has altered their minds, and those that they could not affect are now dead."

Peter waited to see if Jules would ask, and when he did, Peter smiled to himself. They were perfectly mated. He sat down before answering him.

"Her mind is as strong as anyone's I know. No one would be able to erase her memories, nor could they change them. Whoever worked with the others would have known this about her. That is why I believe she was sent to the other house. To be killed."

"So she is still in danger." Peter nodded. "And is that why she was sent here? So that she was more out in the open for them to take care of?"

Peter told him he thought so but wasn't sure. "They want her dead because of the scene she had been working on and the things that had been done to the victims of the house there. The rogue vampire that killed them is still on the loose, as are five more. She has killed one of them, but the others have gone to ground for a reason I do not know." He handed him several pictures. "These are the vampires prior to their going rogue. All of them are fairly young, and all of them are children of Em's brother, Winfred. My connection to them is very weak; I can only find them when they are killing. By then it is nearly too late."

"They don't want what happened to be investigated, so they can continue with their killings." Peter watched the young tiger with a great deal more respect. "Do you think they're the ones that are altering the minds of everyone? Wait, that doesn't explain the paperwork, does it? There is always tons of paperwork when a scene is being worked, I would guess. Hell, you should see what I have to fill out just to send a piece of my work to an overseas buyer. Someone had to take care of all that would come with a crime scene."

Something Peter hadn't thought of. Paperwork. Which meant that there had to be someone on the inside of the police station who was either a vampire or a watcher. And it would have to be someone who knew what to look for as well.

"When she wakes up, we'll have her talk to Brock and Em. They work for the Realm now and can probably help us." Jules flushed when Peter asked him about the *us* part.

"She's my mate and I'll help her. And as of now, she's going to have to put up with me being around a great deal. I'm not going to let her go this easy."

Peter had hoped he'd say that. He reached for his master and told him things were going along as planned. He also told him that someone needed to keep an eye on the elder MacFinley, too. She could be used to harm them.

It is taken care of now. Peter, she will need to have the young tiger move in with them. The house is not safe by half. He agreed, but saying that and having it done was going to be a problem.

Chapter 4

Lenny felt every tear in her body but still needed to open her eyes. She needed to make sure her grandma was all right and to see about being released. She knew she was in the hospital without opening her eyes; after spending eight weeks in one she knew the stench of one like her own apartment. Finally, she opened her eyes only to close them again. It was entirely too bright in the room.

"Let me turn off the light over your face." The light dimmed considerably, and Lenny looked at the man who had spoken. "You've been out for a while. I was beginning to worry."

"Grandma?" Her throat hurt and she was thirsty. The man shoved a straw past her lips and told her to sip slowly. The cold water felt good going in, but almost before she had enough, he took it from her.

"They said only a few sips until they could tell if the medicine they've been giving you didn't make you sick. Did you know that you were allergic to the other stuff?" She knew, but throwing up was worth the three hundred dollar difference in the price of the drugs. "The stuff they're giving you now seems to be much better."

"You a doctor?" He shook his head. "Then what the fuck are you doing here? I need to get home. I can't afford this."

"It's being taken care of."

She didn't like the sound of that and started to tell him so when the door opened and her grandma came in.

"There you are. I've been so worried." She let her kiss her on the forehead, but jerked away when she tried to hug her. The pain that caused made her cry out.

"You need to be still or you'll end up in surgery again." He talked to her like she was five, and she opened her mouth to tear him apart when the door opened again. It was the woman who had helped her the first day she'd been home.

"So you're awake. Good. We were worried when you slept so long. They said it would be a week or so, but we all figured you'd do that by half. I won the bet, by the way. I said four days; everyone else said five or more." She smiled at her. "You need anything, Lenore?"

She growled, a habit she'd picked up from Mason. Pain laced through her heart when she thought of her friend and boss, and it made her a little sharper than she needed to be.

"It's Lenny or MacFinley. It's not Lenore or Ginger or even Red. And what I need is for you all to do is to get the fuck out of here and leave me alone. I want to go home." She looked at her grandma, who was staring at her as if she'd never seen her before. "I'm sorry, Grandma, but I haven't a clue who these people are, and I just want to be left alone."

Her grandma sat down as everyone else left. The man stayed. She could ignore one person but not a room full. Whatever they were giving her for pain was wearing off, and she was having a hard time breathing through the pain. She looked at her grandma and tried to think what to say to her without snapping again.

"I can't afford this and neither can you. Please see if someone will give you paperwork called AMA. It's a form that says I'm leaving against medical advice." Her grandma looked at the man, who nodded. When she left, the man sat in her chair.

"You could have been a great deal more polite about all of this. And as for you leaving, that's not going to happen either. You're still too hurt, and you're still hooked up to the IV that's helping you." She looked at the IV in her hand and pulled it free. He stared at her for several seconds, then laughed.

"I want you to go away." He nodded but didn't move. "I'm in no mood to fuck around, and I certainly can't for the life of me figure out what you want. But you need to leave here before I call security."

"I can call them for you if you'd like, but they won't throw me out. My family owns this place and pays the salary of every person working here. Including the security officers." He leaned back in the chair. "And you're not leaving. There are no AMA papers to be found here, and even if they suddenly appeared, you're still not leaving. As I said before, your bills are being taken care of and that's final."

"Who are you?" She stared at him as he moved closer to her until she could see the flecks of gold in his eyes. She nearly jerked away from him when he lowered his face to hers.

"Don't, Lenny, you'll hurt yourself." She didn't know how to react to the softness of his voice, and waited for him to say something more. When he didn't, she cleared her suddenly dry throat.

"I don't know you." He smiled, and she felt her heart start to race. "You should leave here now. Please."

"See? That wasn't so bad, now was it? I'm Jules Golden and we've met before, but you were in great deal of pain at the time. And I can't leave you, love. Not when I don't know anything about you." Her body began to relax and she looked behind her. The nurse was standing there with a needle, putting something in her IV.

"You distracted me." He nodded and began to fade. "You'll pay for that. I don't like to be fucked with."

"I'm sorry, but you're just too stubborn to keep still until you heal. When you're much better we'll talk some more about your violent tendencies; but for now, you should rest."

Her eyes closed against her will, and the harder she tried to fight the medication, the more it seemed to work its magic. Finally, she let go and slipped into the darkness once again.

~~~

Bronwyn glared at Peter. He was pissing her off, and she was going to knock him on his ass if he didn't tell her what she wanted to know. This beating around the bush and back around again was getting on her last nerve. And the worst part of it was, she was pissed and he wasn't.

"If you tell me one more time that you can't help me, I'm going to make it so you need the help. If she continues to be in so much pain, how will they bond?" She glared harder. "Why can't you give her some of your blood and be done with it?"

"Because she is mine." Bronwyn turned to look at Viktor as he materialized in the room. "When she was laying there dying, I had to save her and gave her several drops of my own blood. She cannot die, but neither can Peter help her now."

"You gave her your blood?" She turned to look at Peter. "Why didn't you tell me that in the first place? I might not have...well, yes I would have, but it would have been nice to know someone is helping her."

"He has been helping her, my lady, but she is not helping herself. Each time she goes against what we've tried to get her to do; she fights us. Her hospital stay was for one more month and then physical therapy, but she came here instead. When we put her to sleep to heal and rest, she will fight us there as well. Even the medications that she is being given in the clinic where she is now, she fights. We can only do so much with her before we are interfering with her life."

Bronwyn snorted. "I don't think you're interfering enough. I can't stand to see her in so much pain. And I can feel it without looking into her mind." He asked her if she had yet. "No. I'm afraid to if you want to know the truth. Whatever did that to her is...he was a vampire, wasn't he?"

"Yes. A rogue like the others your family now looks for. We were late in getting there to help her because she was to wait for backup. But something happened and...." He took a deep breath. "What do you know of her?"

"Nothing really, other than a few tidbits we've found on searches. I know that she and her grandmother had a big fight, her father died in prison, and that she was a detective in Washington. She hurts, but she let Gabby sit on her lap. I don't know why that makes me want to help her more, but there you have it." Bronwyn shivered. "And there is something so haunting about her that terrifies me to no end."

Viktor nodded at Peter, and he left the room. He sat down across from her, and she had a feeling that what he was going to tell her wasn't going to be a bedtime story, but one more horrifying than she'd ever heard in her lifetime. And she had not had an easy life.

"When our Lenore was born, it was under less than ideal circumstances. Her...mother and father were not human, not entirely. Her mother was a watcher, but advanced to vampire when her master took a liking to her in his bed. Do you know what a watcher is?"

She nodded. "Someone who cares for a vampire during the day and brings them a human to feed from when necessary. You? Were you her master?"

"No. I find my own meals, and at my age it is considerably less than a vampire half my age requires. The vampire that she watched was older, but not...he hadn't any sense of worth. He didn't try to make his life better, but would work harder, it seemed, to make his situation worse by doing nothing. He was lazy and his staff was as well." Viktor got up to pace as he continued. "When he found his rest during the day, she would go about finding men to bring into his home. She would lure them to his chamber and allow them to see him and his place of rest. It was dangerous for them both."

"Isn't their resting place like this well-kept secret?" She flushed. "I'm sorry, but you have to know that I never think of you and Peter as vampires. I know that you are, but you're so different than any others I have seen. You're nice."

"We can be." She felt her first curl of fear of the man and wanted to run, but he sat across from her and took

52

her hand, and she felt silly. "You must know something, my dear, that we've told no one else. Peter and I aren't your traditional vampires. We are…more, I would suppose, and not just because of our advanced age. We have powers that we brought with us from our realm that only got stronger when we came here. And as such we are not always nice. We can be quite ruthless and deadly when we need to be. And with this girl, Lenore, we will need to be for her sake."

"What is she? You said she was yours, why? What is she to you that would make you tell me this?" She waited for his answer almost…no, she was terrified of his answer.

"She is the child of a vampire and a half-breed. And before you ask what that is, I shall try to explain." He raised his hands up and suddenly the room was darkened and an image took place in the air in front of her. "This is her mother, Divinity, before she let evil take away her youth. I think she would be going by another name by now; sometimes older vampires feel the need to take on a new identity when they reach certain points in their life. But I digress. She was quite beautiful and wanted by many men. Lenny's father—Grunt was all I knew him by—was such a man."

A man who looked to be huge was there. He had heavy features about his face, full lips, dark brows, and a chin that looked to be sharp. And his teeth…. They looked to be feline. She looked at Viktor.

"He's a shifter." He nodded. "What was his animal? Please tell me he wasn't a tiger. That would just fucking suck big hairy balls."

He laughed at her and shook his head. "You do have an eloquent way with words, do you not? But he was not a tiger, at least not usually. His animal of choice was a

53

leopard. He was a true shifter. And as such could change to whatever he wished, whenever he wished."

"And Lenny, she's a shifter, too?" He shrugged. "You don't know what she is? How is that...?" Something else occurred to her. "Her grandmother isn't her grandmother, is she? She's...you planted her to watch over her for some reason. Her parents, at least one of them, are yours somehow. Or you've given them your blood and you feel responsible for her now."

"You are a great deal smarter than any human I've ever met. And yes, you are correct. Her mother was once saved by me. I gave her my blood and she became my child. I didn't create her into a vampire, but somehow she took on some of the anomalies of one and as such became a rogue like her mate." He watched her, and she had a feeling that he was waiting for her to ask him something.

"Does Lenny know about this?" He said he didn't think so but she may. "Then when do you plan to tell her? Or are you telling her?"

"We were hoping that you might know someone who would...break it to her. Someone that she would not be able to harm, if she did not take the news as well as we hope." Bronwyn wanted to sock the man in the nose. "Someone like you, perhaps?"

"No." He cocked a brow at her. "You do know that she's my future sister-in-law, correct? And for the rest of my life she may hate me because you didn't have the balls to be man enough to tell her that you've been fucking with her life for a long time." She stood up to pace. "Of all the underhanded, slimy, shitty things to do, this rates right up there with the top five of crap I've been asked to do."

"And if she finds out that you knew?" She stopped pacing to stare at him. Anger boiled over her body and she took a step toward him when Peter was suddenly in front of her. It was all she could do not to hurt the men. And while she knew that she could, she wouldn't stoop to their level of playing unfairly.

"You both get out of my house." Neither of them moved, and she looked at Peter. "I'll kill you right now if you don't do that disappearing act right fucking now."

They were both gone before she could blink. Shaking, she sat down and let her mind try and wrap around what they'd just done to her. They'd threatened her. Not with bodily harm but something much worse. They threatened her friendship with someone she admired more than she'd even realized until that moment.

Standing up, she went to see if Gabby was up from her nap and found her playing with her nanny on the floor. After telling her daughter how much she loved her, she told the staff she was going to go to the hospital to see Lenny. It was time she knew the truth about the fucking vampires manipulating her. Instead, she found Jules in the lobby of the clinic, pacing.

"Something wrong?" He looked at her like he was going to explode but took a deep breath instead. She had never seen Jules so...well, anything before. He was the calmest, most laid back person she'd ever met. As far as she knew, he'd never said a cross word to anyone and had been nothing but charming and wonderfully helpful since she'd met him.

"I had to leave." She asked him to sit, and he shook his head. "She is pissed at me again. I've never seen a woman more bent on self-destruction in my entire life as she is. Has she ever heard of simply going with the flow of things?"

"I doubt that in her line of work that really works." She wasn't in a great mood herself and snapped at him. "Sit down, damn it. You're giving me a migraine."

He sat, but he obviously wasn't happy about it. When she sat down, too, it took her several moments to try and explain things to him. She hated to make him the heavy in this, but Lenny would love him. Bronwyn would and could be tossed out of both their lives without a second thought.

"I've just had a very enlightening conversation with Peter and Viktor. It was about Lenny and her...family. She's not human." He looked at her sharply. "They don't know what she is and, frankly, I'm a little pissed about it. They said that they have been watching over her for a while, maybe as long as she's been alive, but that woman who is portraying her grandmother isn't related to her at all. She's been keeping an eye on Lenny for the two of them."

"Why?" She shrugged. "Do you think this whole thing with her and me is real? The reason I ask is because she is...she's not what I want in a mate. Not even close. I know that we get mates that are our other half, but what other half of me do you suppose she makes? I'm a potter, for Christ's sake. I don't get out much other than to shows, and having someone like...well, she's very beautiful, but she's not really my type."

She had thought them oddly paired as well and had said as much to Ryland, but now that Jules thought so, too, she felt better about it. Not that she thought they'd make a shitty couple, but she didn't see Lenny as the art show type of woman, and Jules was certainly not the kickass kind of man who would enjoy going to the shooting range with her and working out. They were ill suited.

"What do you want to do about this?" He got up to pace and now that she'd blown off a little steam, she let him. There was no reason for them both to suffer her bad mood. Not until she needed to hit someone, anyway.

"I'm going to talk to her. See what she wants. It's not like we've done much of anything with her being hurt and all, but...." He looked at her. "Bronwyn, why did you want me to take her to the doctor's office for you?"

Oh well, she thought. "Peter told me you were mates. I asked if it would be all right if I put you two together and he said that would be helpful. So I asked you to do it. I'm sorry, too. Had I known that you felt this way, too, I would never have interfered. I'm sorry."

He nodded and paced. "She's asleep now. I'm going to talk to her and tell her what I think and see what she thinks as well when she wakes up. Maybe something got crossed or...hell, for all we know, she's a really good friend of Peter or Viktor and they wanted her to be a mate to someone, and fixed it so I would be that to her. She even has the house that I've been dreaming of for years."

She didn't know what to say about Peter and Viktor. She had wondered the same thing. But she did feel badly about the house. Jules was the only one who still lived in an apartment, and she'd heard about his perfect house. She'd been to the MacFinley home and had thought the same thing when she'd gotten her first look at the big house, that it was the one Jules wanted.

They went to Lenny's room and watched her sleep as they talked about nothing but mundane things. When the door opened and Nicee walked in, Bronwyn knew that Nicee had heard from either Peter or Viktor. Neither of them said anything, but the tension was there that hadn't been before this. When Bronwyn left, she was standing at the elevator when Nicee came up behind her.

"I'm sorry that I needed to lie to you." Bronwyn didn't answer. "It was...it's important that no one know about our relationship. It's not safe for her."

"Or you?" The woman looked back to the room they'd exited. "You could have told her yourself. At any time over her lifetime someone could have said, 'Hey, not your grandmother, but here's the scoop.' She would have taken it a damned sight better than she will now."

"Probably. But the people who want her are adept at finding things. And if she had told just one person who can't hold their mind as tightly as she can, she would be dead." Bronwyn knew her mind was strong, but she'd not worked very hard to get past her barriers; she hadn't wanted to, as a matter of fact.

The doors to the elevator opened. "But they did find her already, didn't they? Which means, they more than likely know where she is right this minute. What the hell are you going to do about that?"

She stepped in the elevator's yawning opening and felt a moment of unease. She'd hurt the woman, and more than that, she'd been cruel. Bronwyn knew she could be caustic at times, but she was rarely cruel on purpose. When the doors closed, Nicee was still standing there staring at her, and looking as wounded as Bronwyn felt.

Chapter 5

"Where the fuck is she?" Naomi wasn't a patient person in the first place, and this man was standing on the last little reserve she had and was quickly falling over to the point of her killing him. She looked at Milo, her enforcer, her lover, and the man who cared for her.

"She was supposed to be at that old woman's house. This shit hole was supposed to go in, grab her up, and kill off the other bitch. He said she wasn't there." Milo shrugged. "She might have moved in with someone else. They didn't get along before she ran off. Maybe they don't now either."

Milo Hughes had been with her since she'd had him as her watcher about two hundred years ago. They'd been fighting for the rights of her kind for all that time, the rights for vampires, the superior race, to be the only true race on earth. And as soon as the one person who could end their plans of eradicating all humans from this world was dead, Naomi would be just fine. But this person had more lives than a dozen cats. She looked at the man whose name she couldn't think of, then looked at Milo, who reminded her.

"Listen to me, Terrell. You go and find her right now and bring her back to me, or so help me, I will stake you to the ground and watch you fry. If she's not here by Friday, I will find you and kill you." She watched him tremble. "Do you understand me?"

"Yes, mistress. I will find her." He didn't move, and she glanced at Milo. He shrugged again. Wherever he had picked that habit up, she wished to Christ that he'd drop it. It was one of the laziest things she'd ever seen him do.

"Well?"

Terrell glanced up at her from his submissive position of being supine on the floor. She loved the look of pure terror that he'd given her a glimpse of. "I may leave then, mistress?"

She was suddenly wet. His voice, meek and full of fear, made her want to hurt him, made her want to make him bleed on her as she came. When Milo came up behind her and rocked in her ass, she moaned when he squeezed her breast hard enough to make her hurt painfully.

"Let him help us or get him out of here. Either way I'm going to throw you over this desk and fuck you until you hurt." She looked at his face and could see the sadistic look he had, and wanted to beg him to do it. Looking at the man on the floor, she said he was going to help.

"Come here, slave." Terrell sat up and looked at her. "Come here and eat my pussy. And I had better enjoy it or you won't."

He crawled to her, and by the time he got to her, Milo had torn her blouse open and had her skirt up around her waist. Her nipples were being tortured harshly, and she leaned back into his chest. She was so wet that when she opened her legs for Terrell, he licked up her leg to gather her cream. She moaned the moment he put his mouth over her.

"You're going to suck him off while I fuck you as soon as you come, but you'd better not yet." She nodded, unable to speak from what was being done to her. "Do you want him to bite you? Do you want him to drink his fill from your pussy while I watch?"

She cried out her answer and waited for Milo to command the man between her thighs. He walked around to the man and grabbed his head back. Terrell looked like he might have fought Milo, but realized where he was at the last second.

"Feed from her. Bite her clit and drink from her." He nodded but Milo wasn't finished yet. "Then when I tell you to seal the wounds, I want you to take my dick in your mouth and suck me off."

The man looked at the bulge that was clearly outlined on Milo's pants. Terrell licked his lips but looked at her pussy. Either way, the man was going to satisfy one of them shortly, and she only hoped it would be her. When Milo pressed him back to her, she leaned over him and held onto the desk. She rocked into the tongue that swiped over her clit, then screamed when he bit her.

"Christ, that's it, baby. Lean over more." Milo was suddenly behind her at her ass, and she was nearly ready to beg him to take her, but all he did was play. Every time Milo rocked into her, she felt Terrell suck on her harder. When Milo commanded her to come, she grabbed Terrell by the hair and screamed out her release.

Before she was ready for either of them to stop, Milo jerked Terrell away from her and slammed his cock into his mouth. Terrell gagged around him, but Milo continued to pump hard into him. He looked at her with glazed eyes.

"Suck him, now." She nearly fell over her chair to get to the man's cock. As soon as she had him free, she swallowed him. His cock wasn't very large, but it was thick, and she felt him shudder when she licked him from root to tip. She cupped his balls hard as he fucked her mouth. When she tasted his cum on her tongue, Milo jerked her back and she told him to come on her as he fisted his cock. As soon as Milo's first splash of cum hit her body, Terrell stood up and jerked off on her as well.

Hot cum covered her face and breasts. She licked her lips when some touched her there. Before she could enjoy her bounty, Milo told her to stand up. She did what he said, trembling with need, and nearly fell over from it. She held onto the table as Milo ordered Terrell into a new position.

He had Terrell lay on the floor and she was to ride him. As soon as she was settled over his cock, Milo had her lean over. Before she could figure out what he wanted next, he rammed his cock into her ass.

Pain tore through her and with it the best climax she'd ever had. Even as the two of them abused her body, she came twice more. When Milo leaned over her and kissed Terrell, then leaned to his throat, she knew what he was going to do. As soon as his fangs sank into the other man's throat, she bit Terrell as well and drank greedily from him as he bled out.

Lifting her head, she screamed out again when Milo came in her ass. Even as he filled her, she felt the room dim and things fade and blur from the heat of the sun beating on the windows. Her rest time was upon her. Smiling, she knew that when she woke tonight, they'd be in bed together and that the body beneath her getting colder by the second would be just a fun memory in all the men they'd done this same thing to.

"We'll need to find someone else to find her now." She moaned out her agreement as he lifted her, not bothering to open her eyes. "I think I'll send that wolf we heard of a few months ago, the one that is supposed to be the best. I think his name is Lamb. His first name is Sam. You remember hearing about him, don't you? He gets the job done; he's expensive, but he is the best at what he does."

She giggled a little, and he kissed her on the mouth as she lay on the bed. "What do we care? He'll never collect once we get what we want. But he'll have to start from scratch. That fool up there didn't have much and, unfortunately, we didn't get much information from him before we used him up."

Milo pulled her body to his as the sun began to make its way across the sky. He kissed her throat and she gave it to him freely. He was her watcher not a vampire, but he loved to feed from her after sex, so she'd given him the gift of fangs. When he lifted his head and looked at her, she smiled at him.

"You never disappoint me." He smiled at her as she continued. "I love when you take me like you did, make me come like that."

"And I love taking you like that. You're an amazing lover. But you need your rest so that when you wake I'll take you again." She shivered slightly. "I may find us another treat to play with. What would you like, Naomi, male or female?"

Yawning, she told him both. "And make sure that they aren't drugged up if you can. I want to fill up on something more than the cocaine he was full of."

Drugs didn't affect them, but some could leave a bitter, sometimes nasty taste in a vampire's mouth. She rolled to her back as he got up from the bed. She was going to have to talk to him about the men indulging in drugs. It made them stupid and not very useful. He was gone from the room before she could say anything. Yawning again, she let her rest take her.

~~~

Lenny woke and closed her eyes at the brightness of the room. It took her several minutes before she was able to open her eyes fully. She didn't make a sound as she looked around the big room. There were two people in the room with her and only one of them was awake.

"I've come to have a few words with you if you don't mind." Bronwyn Golden didn't look all that happy to see her, either. "I've been given some information about you and I'd like to speak to you about it. I think it sucks that you don't know it already but—"

"No." She tried to sit up, but the pain in her belly tore at her. "I don't think you have anything I want to hear, and even if you did, I don't care to hear it. You're a nice person, I suppose, but I just want to be left alone. I need to be left alone."

"It's about your grandmother." Lenny didn't acknowledge her in any way, but Bronwyn felt she had a story to tell and was going to no matter what she wanted. "What do you know about her?"

The man, Jules she thought his name was, sat up in the chair and watched her as she moved to the edge of the bed. She felt sweat trickle down her back, but needed to get up and get out of there before she racked up another bill she could ill afford. The door she wanted to get to seemed to be miles away rather than the few feet she knew it was. Lenny decided to try and have a conversation that might take her mind off how much she hurt.

"If you mean that she's not my grandma, then I know it. Do I know that someone paid her all this time to care for me? Yep, know that, too." She turned to look at her. "Take all the wind out of your sails there, Mrs. Golden?"

Jules laughed, and both she and Bronwyn glared at him. "You have to admit she's right. You've been burning to tell her since you came here. I, for one, am glad to see someone get one up on you. I never have."

Lenny stood up and had to hold onto the bed for several breaths. She thought that Jules would help her but was glad and disappointed that he didn't. She let go to stagger toward the bathroom and, once there, had to hold onto the sink until she thought she could sit down to pee. As it was, she had too tight a grip on the counter to do anything more than let the pain recede for a little bit anyway.

After going to the bathroom, she hurriedly brushed her teeth. They felt like someone had coated them with fungus and slime and her tongue had a hairy feeling. When she rinsed the brush out after brushing twice more, she knew that whatever happened now on the other side of the door was going to be short and sweet. She didn't have anything left in her. Opening the door, she found Jules standing there. When he scooped her up into his arms and put her on the bed, she barely had time to cry out before a nurse came in.

"You should really wait until someone can come and help you, Mrs. Golden. Next time, just pull the cord and someone will come in. Would you like something for pain now?" Lenny looked around the room and saw that Bronwyn had left. She was about to ask the nurse who she thought was Mrs. Golden when Jules dismissed her. She never even got to tell her that she'd rather they shoved the drugs up their asses because she couldn't afford them anyway.

"She's under some misguided impression that I'm married to one of your family members?" He shook his head. "Then maybe you'd like to explain to me why she referred to me as such. I'm just plain Lenny MacFinley and plan to stay that way."

"How long have you known about your grandmother?" So he was going to ignore her question. Well, she could do that as well.

"Who the fuck do I have to blow to get out of here? I can't afford this place anymore than—" She stopped talking and looked at him. "Did you just growl at me?"

"I did. And you'll not be blowing anyone but me if you feel that need arise again." She frowned at him, not having a clue why he'd thought she was serious. Or for that matter, why he would care. She pulled the sheet over her belly and legs. She wanted the safety of her pants and shirts but didn't think he'd give them to her.

"Why does she think I care about whether or not she's my grandma? And who told her? That's supposed to be the best kept secret in the universe. Someone talking? That vampire maybe, or the woman?" He sat on the edge of the bed and stared at her for several minutes without saying a word. "You know, I can get this sort of titillating conversation from the wall."

"You're my mate. Do you know what that means?" She nodded, then shook her head. "You either do or you don't, Lenore. Which is it? Your understanding of our relationship is going to be much easier to explain if you have at least a little knowledge of what's going on."

"Oh, I understand what it means. I just don't care. I'm not going to be your mate and you aren't going to get the opportunity to try and convince me otherwise." He sat more on the bed and turned to her. "For one thing, if she knows that Nicee MacFinley isn't my real grandma, then you're both aware of what might be going on. Another thing is, I just fucking don't want you near me. You're a tiger. I get that. But there is no fucking way you're going to sleep with me, touch me in any way that is sexual or otherwise, and you sure as shit aren't going to be marking me."

"Why is that?" She didn't understand the question so didn't answer. He was suddenly too close to her and she didn't like it. Moving as far from him as she could, she looked at him when he laughed slightly. There was something very…appealing about him that she didn't want to pursue.

"Why is it you think we're not going to do all that and more? You have something against tigers, or is it men in general you don't care for? Or me?" She bit her inner lip so she couldn't tell him that there wasn't a damned thing wrong with him. "I know, you'd rather I simply walk away because you said so."

He stood up and she tried not to look disappointed. When he reached for his jacket that had been on the back of the chair he'd been sitting in, he turned to smile at her as he pulled it on. She watched as he moved to the door.

"You're going to be much better off this way." She didn't sound all that convinced to herself, but he nodded. "I wasn't much to look at before that vampire tried to slice and dice me, and I sure you wouldn't want to share my bed with me now."

He moved so suddenly that she didn't have time to put her hand up to stop him. He was leaning over her and had her pressed, gently yes, but firmly against the mattress before she could say another word.

"Do you want me to show you how much I want you in my bed? Would you like to see how much I don't care what you look like so long as I can make you mine?" She swallowed hard and felt him move closer to her. "I need to kiss you, Lenore. Take your mouth with mine and taste you on my tongue."

"Please don—" He cut her off. His mouth didn't just kiss her but devastated her, conquered her, and claimed her. His tongue was warm and toyed with her, making her want more than a kiss. His lips were soft, but they were demanding against hers. When he lifted his head, she could see the need in his eyes and thought her own was no less than his reflected back at her. He suckled her lower lip into his mouth and held it there as he looked deep into her eyes. She moaned when he let it go.

"Do you have any idea how delicious you taste?" She shook her head. "Like hot, wet sex on silk sheets. Like warmed honey." He smiled at her but didn't move.

"Why did you kiss me?" He leaned close to her again and licked along her lips to her chin and down to her throat. When he nipped gently at her skin, she moaned and tilted her head. He bit harder and she shifted on the bed, suddenly feeling warm all over. She moaned when he bit her a third time.

"Why not?" He whispered against her throat. She wanted him to stop but couldn't for the life of her remember why. She'd had a good reason, but now all she could think about was what he was doing and how good it was feeling.

When he lifted his head this time, she saw a drop of blood on his lip and pulled him down to lick it off. As soon as her mouth touched his, he moaned and speared his tongue into her mouth, and danced it along hers. She was curling her hand into his hair to bring him as close as she could when he stiffened.

"What is it?" He lifted his head. Then after a brief but no less thorough kiss, he pulled from her body, stood next to the bed, and she could see his erection. She nearly reached out to cup him in her hand when the door opened behind him.

"Hello." The man standing there didn't seem the least bit surprised to see to see Jules near the bed. In fact, he was laughing and not trying very hard to hide it. "I'm his big brother, Ryland. You must be Lenore."

"I'm Lenny. Lenny MacFinley. You're that woman's husband or mate or whatever, Bronwyn. You're going to be just as annoying as she is, aren't you?" He nodded. "She's a pain in the ass, too."

"Not that I'm agreeing with you, but she can be a little on the stern side. How are you feeling today? Ready to come home with us?" She glanced at Jules, then back at Ryland when nothing was forthcoming. "He didn't tell you?"

"No. He was busy doing other things." She flushed a little when she realized what she'd said, and glared at Ryland when he laughed. "I'm not going anywhere with either of you. I have a perfectly good home, with all of it set up for me until I can get back to my apartment. And then once there, I plan to live my life to the fullest."

Jules growled and the hair on the back of her neck stood up and danced. She looked at him and then at his brother. She knew that neither of them was human and she knew what they were. Something tugged at her memory, but she couldn't put her finger on it. All she knew was she wanted these men gone.

Bits and pieces about the night she'd been hurt came to her at odd times. There was Mason standing at the top of the stairs with a man sucking on his neck. That frightened her a great deal, but she knew that it wasn't the worst. Whatever she'd hidden away from, according to the doctors she'd seen back home, was going to surface when she would least expect it. They'd also told her that when she remembered anything, she was to call them immediately. She hadn't called anyone as yet and had no intentions of doing so either.

She also remembered the man who had stood over her, cutting into her body with nothing more than his finger. He had spoken to her, but she couldn't remember what he'd said until Jules had growled just now.

"He said that he was there only to kill me. But to have me for all time would be more than the payment they were getting to kill me. He said *she* wanted me dead. Then he growled." Lenny looked at both men, who seemed to be frozen in place. Fear of the unknown scared her, but their look, the one that they were giving her now, made her think that they knew a great deal more about what had happened than she remembered or even wanted to. She shifted on the bed and pulled the cord that was wrapped on the railing around her.

"Yes." The disembodied voice sounded loud in the big room. "Jules, did you need something else?"

She looked at Jules and tried to tamp down the feelings of jealously that ran though her. "I'd like to leave now. Can you find my doctor so that I can get the hell out of here?"

"You've already been released, Mrs. Golden. I have all your meds and paperwork here. I was just bringing it in for the male." She looked at Ryland, who shrugged.

"I'm the male of our family." She didn't really need him to explain, but he seemed to need to tell her. "The leader of a group of tigers is called a male. A group of us is called an ambush or streak, which is what we prefer. And I thought that Jules had told you while your home is being outfitted for a security system, you're staying with us. So is he."

"I can't afford a security system put in even if it's a free mutt from the pound, and I know damn good and well I didn't approve of one." Ryland looked at Jules. Then she did as well. "You did this?"

"You're not safe there." She wanted to scream at him that she hadn't been safe anywhere even when she had a gun, but he continued before she could. "It's not a mutt but a good system being put in. I have the same one at my studio. There is no reason for you to worry about money any longer. As for you returning to Washington, that's not going to happen either, unless we go there together, and I can't do that right now. I've taken care of your things in that tiny little place you lived in, too. If I have to have you as a mate, you'll have to adjust to my way of life since yours seems to be finished there."

Lenny didn't move, but she saw Ryland backing up. *Smart man.* As soon as he stepped out the door, she moved to the side of the bed to get up. Jules moved to stand in front of her.

"Get away from me." He took a step back and frowned at her. "You touch me again and I will kill you."

"You can't be pissed off because I've taken care of you." She stood up and didn't know if it was being pissed that made her move better, but she was getting out of there before it was too late and she really did kill the man.

When he stepped to her again, she drew back her fist and hit him right in the face. She watched as he fell back, his nose and mouth already pouring blood. When he hit the floor and took a bounce, she went to the little closet she'd noticed earlier and pulled on her clothes. They were blood covered, but at that point she didn't give a fuck. Changing in the bathroom as quickly as she could without hurting herself more, she was out and standing in the hall within five minutes. Ryland was leaning against the desk.

"Do you need a ride back to your house?" She nodded. "Come on then. Jules will be pissed when he gets up, but he deserves whatever you did to him for being a dick."

She didn't say a single word until he dropped her off other than to thank him. She told the three men there, all of them Goldens, she had no doubt that their services were no longer needed. She told them that she'd shoot the first one she saw if they weren't gone by the time she got her gun. Ryland nodded at them, and she went inside. *Fucking idiot men* was all she could think about before she burst into tears.

Chapter 6

Lamb moved along the property of the woman. There was a great deal of scent around and he had to be extra careful not to remark some of the wolf ones. Damn, but there had been a lot of different animals where he was currently standing. Taking another deep breath and trying to separate their scents from the woman's, he couldn't find her. But it mattered little to him.

He was going inside tonight to kill her, and anyone else that got in his way. He had a job to do and he'd be damned if he ended up like his predecessor. Dead was not what he wanted to wear today. Laughing to himself, he moved closer to the house and stopped when he saw the panther. Fuck.

He watched the sleek animal and had to calm his wolf into waiting. He had no idea if there was a second one, and he wasn't sure who the big cat was. When a tiger and a large black bear moved to stand beside the panther, Lamb lay down and slowed his breathing to almost a stop. This was no fucking good.

He could beat one of the animals, sure. Maybe even hurt another, but not with the three of them working together. And he had a feeling that they were, too. He watched them for several minutes, wondering if they'd move out to do another check, but when the big bear moved up to the porch and sat down, he knew they were settling in for the night. He moved back slowly and left the property, glad for the other scents because they more than likely hid him as well.

He was pulling on his shirt when his cell phone rang. He almost ignored it because it would only be one of three people. His mom, who he loved dearly but didn't feel like lying to right now, his brother wanting to borrow money again, or the fucking vampire. He glanced at the ID and saw the vamp's name flash every time it vibrated.

"Yeah." He hated this man more than he could say, and he was pretty sure there was no love lost between the two of them. When there was no immediate answer, he hung up. He didn't have time for mind games, and he certainly didn't want to play them with a fucking prick.

The next time it rang he was driving. One thing he'd learned over the years was don't text and drive and don't drive pissed. And he was reasonably sure he was going to be pissed when he spoke to him. Pulling over when it went to voicemail, he pulled up the message. Laughing, he replayed it.

You mother fucking son of a bitch fucktard. When I call you you'd better never hang up on me again or so help me I will hunt you down and drain you just because I can. Now call me back within the next five minutes, or so help me you will not live long enough to draw your next breath.

Lamb tossed the phone on the seat next to him and pulled into traffic again. This was the reason he never had personal contact with the people who hired him. Especially with a vampire who had a reputation of killing off those who didn't serve him well. Lamb had never trusted vampires in the first place, and this one less so. He moved toward one of his many hidey holes and went inside. He was lying back on his lumpy mattress when his phone rang again.

Closing his eyes, he wasn't surprised to hear it ring almost as soon as it stopped ringing. He'd told the vampire that he'd get back with him when he had some information. He didn't say he'd give him updates every ten minutes, and he wouldn't even if the guy had demanded it. He had more important things to do with his time. Like not giving updates every ten. Laughing, he rolled to his side.

The woman had to be something special to have someone call him in. Lamb wasn't known for his tactics, nor was he all that gentle when he was ordered to kill. He had in the recent past gone into a large shopping market, walked up behind a target, and snapped their neck as they were reaching for the milk. But he did get the job done.

Long ago, he'd not had such a great reputation. He'd been known as a sloppy agent, as well as somewhat of a hot head. He was still a hot head, but he tried to find humor in what was going on around him instead of the bullshit silver lining his mom had told him to look for. What the fuck was silver going to do to help a fucking wolf, anyway?

And he now realized that he had been lucky that he'd never been killed, either by the target or the people he'd worked for. He'd been lazy. He'd finish a job when it suited him, killed without much care for what was happening around him, and didn't give two shits if he was drunk when he did the hits. Which by his estimations he was most of the time. Yeah, he had been lucky that no one had killed him or he'd killed himself.

But things had changed when he'd killed a guy about ten years ago in front of the man's kid. The little boy couldn't have been more than three or four, but he'd watched him do it. And for as long as he lived he'd never forget the kid's face when the man he'd known as his daddy for his entire life just dropped to the ground in front of him. To this day at odd moments he'd see the kid's haunted look. He wondered what the boy was doing now or if he was seeing a head doctor.

The phone stopped ringing around sunrise. It had taken the vampire longer than he'd thought to give up, and San wondered if he had only stopped because of the sun or he realized that pissing him off wasn't a way to get the job done. Either way he was glad for the quiet. He supposed he could have gotten up and turned the ringer off, but what fun would that have been? Closing his eyes, Sam went to sleep. He had a big night ahead of him and he wanted to be on his best when he murdered the girl and whatever animal was around.

~~~

She felt like shit. Lenny looked in the mirror over the sink and thought she looked it as well. There were dark circles under her eyes, as well as them being bloodshot and puffy. Taking a wet cloth, she pressed it over her face and tried to reason with herself that she could go back to Washington and get around without much in the way of pain. It wasn't working, but she did have a nice argument going with herself when her grandma knocked on the door.

"There's a couple here to see you. They said they want to talk to you about what happened in Washington. They said that they have some information that might help you." She didn't answer her because frankly, she was trying her best not to tell her to go away and leave her to her pain. "Lenny?"

"Tell them I'll be right out, but tell them I don't remember what happened with me and nothing on Mason either." She said she would and asked if she wanted anything to eat. "No thanks. Just some tea if you don't mind."

By the time she'd pulled on her pants and a clean shirt, she was hurting again. But she wasn't going to take any more of the drugs unless the pain was just too bad to breathe through. She hated feeling all doped up, and didn't want to become dependent on them either. She had enough shit going on. And today she was going to take a shower and have a good look at herself. She'd never seen much more than the wounds on her left leg, and those were bad enough.

The couple sitting in her grandma's living room looked like they had stepped off the Rich and Famous program her grandma watched. Not to mention they looked like they had been sculpted from some kind of god and goddess. She pulled her sweatshirt away from her body to hide what she was sure would terrify them.

"Hello, Lenny. I'm Brock and this is my wife Em. We're here to get some information from you on what happened in Washington when you were hurt. We also have a little bit to share with you, too." He glanced at his wife, who winked at him. "Em and I work for a very top agency that deals in paranormal bad guys. We hoped that you could help us get them off the streets."

"I'm neither stupid nor one of your idiot brothers, Mr. Golden, so I would appreciate it if you didn't treat me like it. If you looked any more like the older one, I'd think you were cloned. What do you want?" He leaned back on the couch and smiled at her. "You might be thought of as charming, but I've never been accused of that in my life. Spill it, then go."

"Okay. Em and I work for the Holders of the Realm, a large network of supernaturals that hunt down rogues and kill them so that the world, this one and others, are safe from them. We've been notified that you might have had an encounter with one, and we'd like to see if you can help us catch them."

She took several low, long breaths. She'd never heard of this group, but didn't doubt that there really was one. This man looked like he would kick some major ass with a vamp and, for that matter, so did the woman. But she had nothing to give them.

"I don't remember what happened. Some bits and pieces come to me at odd times, but I don't know what happened. They said I had a heart attack and that what little I do remember is part of the drugs they gave me when I fell down the stairs." She looked away from them before they could see how much it bothered her that someone was lying to her about what had happened. "You'll just have to trust me when I tell you I have nothing to tell."

"But you do, don't you?" Lenny looked at Em as she smiled. "You know a great deal about what happened, but for whatever reason you're not sharing. You don't trust us, which I can understand. You've just met us. You especially don't trust those people in the hospital. I doubt you've even told the ones in Washington that you're even remembering a little of what happened, have you? Did they tell you to call them when you had a memory come back to you? Why is it you suppose they want to know?

Or do you believe you are only alive because of the fact that you can't remember?"

Lenny stood up and glared at the two of them. "Did you hear me? I don't remember anything to help you. I've been ill, and I just want to get well enough to go back to my other life. Try to pick up the pieces and move on."

"How bad did he hurt you?" She looked at Brock, thinking he was talking about his brother and yesterday. "The vampire that you killed, how badly did he cut you up?"

"I fell." He shook his head and stood up. She took a step back from him and reached for the gun that was no longer a part of her clothing. "You need to leave."

Moving slowly, he reached into his back and pulled out a gun. He didn't take his eyes off hers, but she heard him take out the clip and pull the slide back. He touched her hand gently and put her hand around the butt. When she looked down, he put the clip into her other hand and still held the gun in her first one.

"It's loaded with silver. And before we leave here, I'll make sure you have enough to reload it when you need to." She looked up at him. "I'm not going to hurt you, Lenny. We're only here to help you."

"He said he was supposed to kill me." He nodded and sat back down beside his wife. "I don't remember…there are so many gaps in my memory that I'm not sure what's true or not."

"They said you'd gone there on your own. You said when they brought you in that you'd gotten a call and had gone there with Joseph Mason. Can you tell me where you were when the call came to you?" She shook her head and Em smiled as she continued. "It's okay if you don't. We'll get to it."

"No, I mean the call didn't come to me. Mason…Mason came to me. He was…someone else was supposed to go with me. I don't remember who, but…." Her head began to pound again, but she wanted to remember. "Mason told me that dispatch had told him, and that whoever I was supposed to go with—Rice…. His name was Rice, and he was my partner. But something happened to him and he didn't go. Mason and I went to the house. He said that he had the address of a murder. A murder like the one—"

Her head exploded in pain, and she felt someone push her head back and put a cold cloth over her face. Blood entered her mouth, and she knew that her nose had started to bleed again. She tried hard to not beg someone to give her something for the pain. Instead, she felt ice run over her wrist, and the pain receded almost immediately.

"It's a trick that Brock's mom showed me. She said it's a cure for everything. I believe her, and have taken to carrying around icepacks that you break to make work just to try it on whatever happens. So far, so good." Em smiled at her. "You'll love her, too. She's an amazing woman. Scary, too, but really nice. What do you think of Jules?"

The quick subject change threw her off or she was sure she would have answered a lot differently. "He's a bossy know-it-all bastard that needs to tone it down a bit or someone, namely me, will take him down a notch or two."

She looked at Brock when he laughed. He was nodding at her when her grandma came in bearing a large pizza pan with cups and other things on it. Lenny grinned when she saw the lacy doilies on it to probably hide the fact that it wasn't a serving tray, but neither Brock nor Em seemed to care. They dove into the cookies and cheese and crackers like they'd not eaten for a month.

"Man, I love sugar cookies." Brock was shoving two more in his mouth as he gulped down the iced tea Grandma had handed him. "Do you know how long it's been since I've had one? My mom hates them, and Em and I have barely enough time to sleep, much less bake. These are amazing."

Her grandma brought out the large container that she'd filled with the cookies she'd baked yesterday and told Brock that she'd make sure he had some to take home. He told her that he'd be forever in her debt, and ate a dozen more before he sat back and smiled contently. Em had eaten just as much as her husband, while Lenny had sipped her tea.

"You'll need to eat more when you and Jules come to be mated. There's a lot of energy burned up between newly formed couples." When Brock wiggled his brows at her, she flushed. "I heard what he said to you at the hospital."

Lenny nodded. "He's nothing to me. As soon as I'm able, I'm thinking within the week, I'm going back to Washington to try and see if I can find a job working with the police. They won't let me go out on the cases anymore, but maybe they can—" Brock and Em both were shaking their heads. "What do you mean 'no'?"

"You can't go back, and they aren't going to hire you at any job. You're marked. And not just as Jules's mate. You do know that the mark he gave you will be seen by all tigers, and if there are any among your other detectives or even officers, they won't work with you." She asked him what he was talking about by saying she was marked. "They think you killed Mason. And those that don't think you're insane and should be locked up before you hurt yourself will never trust you with their back. They won't accept you back because no one would back you up. Or did you mean the mark that Jules gave you?"

She was pretty sure he knew just what she meant. Lenny thought about the fact that her fellow officers thought she'd killed her friend, but the fact of being marked by Jules still burned in her mind. He had marked her? How the hell had...the bite he'd given her in the hospital.

"He kissed me and then he nipped at my shoulder." Brock and Em both nodded. "He marked me as what? You said mate. Is that all?"

"Not really. He's started to claim you. And if he has sex with you in any way, he will claim you. If you bite him, then all bets are off, kiddo. He owns you as well as you do him." Lenny stood up but had to sit down quickly. Pain shot through her and she didn't want to fall. She had a tiger to kill.

"And if I tell him to back the fuck up and leave me alone, that won't work either, will it?" Em shook her head. "I'm really sorry then. I'm going to have to kill him. Prison will be better in the long run than having him speak to me the way he did. And if he thinks I'm going to be a doormat for him, he's a fucking idiot."

Neither of them said anything for several minutes as they finished their tea. Then Em looked at her and asked her about Rice. The question had been simple, too.

"He was a moron. He actually raised his hand to ask me a question, like we were in grade school. But we got him at the scene. He had a weak stomach, and every time he came into one of the rooms where I was working, one of us would make a gagging noise or show him some other body part that we'd found. It wasn't meant to be showing disrespect to the dead, but he was messing up the crime scene every time he fell over into the blood and—" Lenny looked at Em. "There was blood. I'm not...I can't remember where it had come from, but I was point on the scene."

"Think about Rice, not the scene." Lenny nodded at Brock. "Close your eyes and think about what he was doing the first time you saw him."

Lenny closed her eyes, thankful for the small memories she could get now and in some sort of order. "He was standing by a car. I think he was going to go with me to the scene. He had on a pair of black pants with a shiny belt and a white shirt. You never wear a white shirt to homicide. It will be covered in something as soon as you enter the crime scene."

"What else?" Brock's voice sounded far away now and she let herself be comforted by it. She liked Jules's better, but was not particularly fond of what drivel spilled from his lips. The man was an ass and—Brock said her name softly.

"My previous partner had transferred out. His wife, he said, wanted him to be safer. He told me on his last day it was because I was a control freak and he couldn't stand to play second fiddle to me. I had a feeling that was it, but it didn't matter. He'd nearly gotten us killed when he'd pulled into an intersection going ninety chasing a bank robber and not waiting a second to see if it was clear." She shifted on the couch. "Rice was on the rotation to ride with me. He was the mayor's nephew and Mason told me...later I think...that he'd put him with me because he knew I'd run him through enough horseshit to make him quit. I think he did."

Images flipped though her mind like a fast-moving picture album; Mason standing above her looking happy with himself; a hand, severed from a male, being held by someone else; a shoe lying in a doorway. Lenny felt her head begin to pound again and opened her eyes. She was surprised to see that at some point Jules had come in, and she hated that her heart took a weird leap in her chest.

"I think we have enough now to get a start. If you remember any more, don't hesitate to give us a call and let us know." As Brock moved out of the house, Em continued speaking. "As we get information, too, we'll pass it along. It might trigger you to remember something else or nothing at all. But we'll be nearby."

Brock handed her three boxes of ammo for the gun and she looked up at him, surprised. "There are several rogues out there that might come around. I'm not sure they will, but this will give you a chance to take them out before we get here. The silver works on wolves as well, but not tigers. Not unless you shoot them in the head or heart."

He was still laughing when he and Em left. She started for her bedroom, hoping that Jules would get the hint and leave, but he followed her. She pulled some clothes off the chair that her grandma had brought from her suitcase. She was taking a shower and to hell with him.

"Are you not speaking to me?" She didn't even turn around to look at him. "You should know that I don't want a mate. Not like you anyway, but I guess we're stuck with each other."

She paused long enough to count to ten before going to the bathroom door. If he was still standing there when he came out, she was going to shoot him in the head.

She'd had enough of him today already. When he touched her shoulder, she thought about three things at once; hit him, which seemed her best course of action; ignore him…so not going to happen with him breathing on her and scorching her skin like he was; or simply walk away. She tightened her clothes in her hands and walked into the bathroom. It was by far the hardest few steps she'd ever taken.

Turning on the water, she stripped off her shirt and stepped under the cold spray, and never opened her eyes the entire time. She was hurting enough without seeing what had happened to her just yet. And realizing that she'd forgotten to take off the bandages only made her madder at the large tiger outside. By the time she was finished, her hair and body were clean, but she was dripping blood from the wet gauze. Another thing to blame on Jules.

Chapter 7

Naomi looked around the devastation that was once her lovely office. She'd been more than a little pissed off, and it showed in every broken piece of pottery she'd been collecting over the centuries, as well as the new office equipment that had only been installed the month before. She sat down on what she thought was once a chair and tried to regain some control. When the vampire walked in without bothering to knock, she flew at him and wrapped her hand around his throat so quickly she doubted that he had time to blink.

"What have I told you about coming into my home without permission?" Truman Smith glared just long enough for her to think she'd imagined it, but still she shook him. "You've been told several hundred times in our short acquaintance to knock, but you continue to simply have bad manners and piss me off."

"I'm sorry, my lady. I came to talk to you about the wolf you hired." She tossed him across the room, sighed when he hit the only piece of art that had survived her wrath, and sat back down. He was just picking himself up when Milo came into the room.

He didn't say anything but looked at her oddly. So the fuck what? It was her house, and if she wanted to trash it daily, it was her business, not his. He leaned against the mantel and nodded for the other vampire to speak.

"He's been to the house that the girl lives at, but he didn't kill her. I saw her and that old broad walking around the house. She's had a couple of tigers inside, but they left a long time ago. One of them stayed for a while, but he never came out while I was there. When I took a leak, he was gone when I came back. But the wolf, I could smell him at the house." He looked confused for several seconds. "I think I smelled a bear, too, and a bunch of other wolves, so I'm not sure it was him. It could have been a lot of others."

He nodded, and Naomi started to rise up and kill the dumbass, but Milo spoke first. "You say a lot of others. You mean other wolves? There were other wolves on the property?"

"Yeah. And some…I swear I smelled that bear and cat. Not like the tigers smell when you showed me, but like other cats. You think they have a kitten or something?" Naomi shook her head. Where the fuck had this idiot come from? Then she remembered.

He and three other vampires, all of them fairly young, had come to her just after their master had been killed. They were not only lost but also ignorant of what to do to survive. Of course, it hadn't taken her long to figure out they were just plain ignorant, but that was beside the point. They had come in handy so far in tracking the girl.

"I'm betting it's some of those Golden men. I've heard that they've taken a special interest in the girl. Probably one of them is sniffing around her." Naomi mentally rolled her eyes. Sometimes Milo still sounded like the dock worker she'd taken as her lover all those decades ago.

For her own peace of mind, she asked if they were the panthers or the tigers. She hated both kinds of cats, but tigers terrified her to no end. She didn't even know why, but whenever she thought of coming into contact with one of them, she felt her skin crawl. She shivered when Milo told her it was the tigers.

"Well, if the fucking wolf would ever call us back, we can get some things taken care of. Or at least some answers." She looked around the room again. "He's going to pay for not calling me back when we see him."

Truman nodded and slowly started for the door. The sun was still hours away yet, and she wanted to play, but Milo told him to leave now, and she looked at her lover, disappointed. He sat down but made no move to touch her.

"You should know that I've heard your good friend Viktor is around again." Every nerve in her body seemed to freeze. "He was spotted at a flower shop about two weeks ago with some other being that I can't figure out what she is."

"How did you find out?" She tried to act as if it didn't matter to her if he was close, but Milo knew the history between them and wasn't fooled for a minute. When he laughed, she saw red.

"You might as well just face the fact that you still want him and move on. He certainly has if the way he was laughing it up with that other being is any indication." She tried to take shallow breaths to curb her temper, but he just wouldn't shut the fuck up. The more he said, the hotter she got until she turned and attacked.

"They were all chummy and touching each other. I think she was a tiger but a lot more. I'm not sure. Anyway, when they left together, I followed. He took her to lunch. Then they went to a studio downtown. I'm betting he bought her the nice piece in the front lobby because he put it in her car when she left."

He wasn't prepared for her, so she was winning before he could gather his strength. By the time she'd sank her fangs deep into his throat, she was beyond caring that this man was all that lay between her and danger. She wanted him to pay for what he'd made her feel, and all the other pent-up rage she'd had since waking. By the time she lifted her head, he was too far gone for her to save, and without even trying, she lifted from his body and walked away. By the time she'd gone to her lower levels to lock herself in, he was dead.

Smiling for the first time since she'd found out that the girl was close, she went to bed just after midnight, long before she normally did, and closed her eyes. Tomorrow she was going to find the wolf and replace Milo. Enough of this bullshit waiting around for her to come to find her.

Mommy was going to kill her daughter if it was the last thing she did.

~~~

Jules was waiting for his replacement to show up when he noticed the wolf again. It wasn't unusual with this many weres helping them keep an eye on Lenny's home that he'd not know one or two of them, but this one was different than the others.

For one, he never engaged in much conversation, which he supposed was the man's biggest giveaway. Wolves were pack animals and needed the company of others. Secondly, and he thought most importantly, he seemed to be watching the house more than he was the grounds. Jules started for him when he felt the first bit of unease. He turned to the house to see if he could find anything.

Other than the giant bear seemingly sleeping on the porch, there was nothing. Going back the way he'd come, he called for Ryland, who was patrolling the grounds with him tonight, to go and find the wolf.

He's just sitting there and watching and not doing what he should be doing. Not watching the grounds like I would think he should, but the window where Lenny is sleeping. Ryland laughed. *I don't know a great deal about tracking like the rest of you, but I know when I can feel things are off.*

She's going to kick your ass if you go into her house again. I'm pretty sure that she made her position pretty clear today. Jules didn't stop walking toward the house. *She's not going to be any happier with you when she finds out for the past few nights you've called in every favor you've had in getting other weres here to help.*

She'll get over it. Besides, if she had spoken to me today, I would have told her what was going on. The closer he got to the house, the more fearful he became. Then he realized it wasn't him but her he was feeling. He was just telling his brother something was off when he heard her scream. Not bothering with shifting and going in the front door, he crashed through the window to her room.

Her screams tore through him, as did the emotions that went with them. They weren't just like fear, but of terror like nothing he'd ever known before. Even as he scanned the room, he knew she was alone, and when the door opened suddenly and a flash hit his eyes, he snarled at whoever was there.

"Dreams. Wake her." Nicee had entered and the flash was a light she carried. She yelled at him again to wake Lenny up. He leapt up on the bed as he shifted to human and took her hands, which were flaying at him, and held them above her head. He tried his best not to hurt her, but if she screamed again like that, he wasn't sure he could handle it. When she started sobbing and looked at him, he kissed her on the mouth. It was the only thing he could think of.

When he lifted his head, she was staring up at him, and he let her hands go. He heard Nicee leave the room and tell someone that he had it under control. The slight breeze across his ass made him realize he was naked.

"He took him. When Mason went into the house, someone jerked him into the house so quickly that he lost his shoe. He lost his shoe." Jules nodded at her. "I remember now. All of it. I remember that I had been working another crime scene and that there were five bodies messed up, but the male had been torn to pieces."

She wrapped her arms around his shoulders and held him as she shuddered. She started her story over and over. He let her know that now that she remembered, she'd line it all up and tell it to his brother in the right order. He could feel her mind working out what she had seen as opposed to what she'd thought she'd seen. He held her, never letting go of her, holding her to him until she was finished.

When she curled her fingers into his back he watched her mouth. She had stopped talking a little after the sun peaked in the sky. He wanted desperately to lean down and kiss her, then bury himself deep inside of her.

"You are probably uncomfortable." He didn't know how to answer that, so he didn't. "I'm really sorry. I'm not a cry baby. But the dreams...I guess I needed the push your brother gave me today. Well, yesterday, I guess now."

"He said that you remembered a little." She nodded, and he could feel her breasts move against his chest. "I talked to him and Em last night before I came over here and...."

She licked her lips. Jules watched as her tongue moved from one side of her luscious mouth to the other. He wasn't sure if he'd seen anything more beautiful or more erotic in his entire life. Then she pulled her lower lip into her mouth and bit it.

"Lenny, I want to kiss you. I actually want to do a great deal more than that, but kissing you won't kill me." She smiled at him, and he thought maybe he was going to die anyway.

Lowering his head slowly, he moved his hands down her body to her waist. He could feel the bandages there and thought they'd help him remember not to hurt her. But when he touched his mouth to hers, nothing mattered but taking more of her into him.

Her tongue slid around his as soon as he deepened the kiss. Moaning when she cupped the back of his head, Jules slid his hand under her ass and lifted her into his cock. She jerked her mouth from his and moaned low. He nipped at her exposed throat, licked along the vein there, and suckled in her pounding pulse. He wanted to bite her, sink his teeth into her as much as he did his cock. Moaning again, he moved his way down her chest to her breast. Sucking at the tip hard through the sheet that kept him from her, he rocked harder into her. Lenny moaned his name.

He heard a slight noise and lifted his head. Growling low in his throat, he looked behind him at the broken window, as well as Ryland standing there with his back to him. He would gladly kill him right now.

You're not being very discreet there, brother dear. Anyone in the yard can see the two of you. Is that what you want?

Jules growled again and looked back at Lenny. Her eyes were glazed over and there were bite marks all along her throat and down to where her breast was hidden beneath her sheet. He had a feeling that she was as naked as he was and wanted to snarl at the way things were right now. But as much as he hated to admit it, Ryland was right. Their first time together shouldn't be done where everyone could watch them.

I'll need help getting the window fixed and some clothes. He saw a small duffle slide across the floor. *Thanks. Christ, Ryland, I don't want to leave her right now.*

But you have to. Come on. I'll walk away, but you have to get going. There are things you have to know as well about the wolf from earlier.

"There are others too close right now for me to finish what we've started." Lenny looked at him without focusing. He wanted to make her look like that a great deal more, like she'd just been made love to hard and quick. "I have to get up."

She nodded and shifted in the bed, and his cock did as well. He could feel how hot she was, how wet the sheet was between them. He groaned hard and rocked again. When she rolled her hips up to meet him, he buried his face in her neck and did bite her. She cried out but didn't pull away as her hot blood filled his mouth.

Lifting his head again, he looked down at her. Blood trickled from the wound he'd given her and he wanted to take her more than ever before. But he had to get up because if he didn't, there wouldn't be a person within a hundred miles that wouldn't know that he'd claimed her. He lifted his body from hers and licked the wound at her throat. She shivered beneath him and moaned when she looked down their bodies.

"You're naked." He nodded. "You should…how did you…Christ, you're beautiful. And so hard. I want to touch you."

He leapt from the bed before her fingers touched him. "You touch me and I'm not going to be able to stop." His cock ached in the cool morning air. "Do you have any idea how much I want to say fuck the open window and take you? How much I want to suckle at your nipples while I move in and out of you?"

She nodded. "Yes. I want the same thing, too, right now, but we can't. We're not…I'm not going to be what you want, Jules. I can't. I have to figure out who killed Mason and why they did this to me."

He took a step toward her to show her how much she could be what he wanted, what she wanted, but she put up her hand. "You're my mate, Lenny. Now that I've bitten you, you're not going to leave me. I want you to let me take care of this for you."

She laughed and got out of the bed with a sheet wrapped around her. She went into the bathroom without a word. He felt his anger surge forth. Before he opened his mouth again or followed her, he felt Bronwyn touch his mind. She was laughing and that made him nearly snarl at her.

You do and I'll hurt you in ways that your children's children will feel. Get dressed and get out of the house. You're going to fuck things up worse if you don't. She was suddenly pissed, but so was he.

You can't tell me what to do with my mate. You have no rights – His head exploded in pain. Blood dripped to the floor when he went to his knees as his belly tightened up, too. He was feeling the darkness swamp him, then suddenly he was free.

You still think I can't? Get dressed and leave her alone. She's had...Christ, Jules, where the fuck did you get these ideas in your head that she would simply do what you wanted because you're her mate? You fucking idiot, she's stronger than you'll be on your best day, and a lot smarter in thinking this won't work if you continue treating her like a thing rather than a mate.

She's mine. And as such, it is my duty —

Fuck your duty, you moron. She's going to leave you, and what the fuck are you going to do then? Follow her? Make her have to shoot you? She will. I have no doubt about that at all. Now this is the last time I'm going to say this. Get your fucking clothes on and get out of that house. I'm waiting for you. He wanted to tell her to go to hell but she simply tightened around his head a little again and he reached for his clothes. *She's hurting. Not badly but enough. And she's afraid of you. Are you happy about that?*

I didn't mean to frighten her. But she needs to learn that she can't just go out and do things on her own anymore. Bronwyn laughed at him. *You wouldn't think this was so fucking funny if that was Ryland in there.*

No, but Ryland wouldn't be treating me like some sort of idiot like you are her. Have you once asked her what she wants or needs? Did you ask her or even explain to her what you did to her when you bit her? I know you didn't. He flushed, knowing that by law, streak law, he should have. *You are a Neanderthal. A pigheaded, moronic, dumbassed Neanderthal, and I'm ashamed to call you family right now.*

He stopped pulling on his socks. Neanderthal? He was a little old fashioned, but not that bad, was he? He moved out of the house by the window he'd come through and looked at his brothers standing next to a truck. It was loaded with boards, and he could see other things to fix the damage he'd done as well. When he glanced back into the room, he saw Lenny's grandmother speaking to Lenny, but his brother slapped him on the back before he could figure out what they were saying. He looked at Alistair, then at Bronwyn as she stood talking to Ryland.

"You really fucked up this time. I've never seen Bronwyn so pissed off before. Glad it's you and not me. I think she's planning to castrate you." Both of them cupped their cocks and balls when she started toward them. "This is the first time since I've discovered the law that I'll be glad to be somewhere where you're not. She's going to kill you."

When she stood in front of him he tried to stand his ground, but she was his female to the streak, and he knew as well as his cat did that he'd handled the situation wrong. As he dropped to one knee in front of her and bowed his head, his cat moved along his skin. The thing was, his cat might be agreeing with his female, but Jules still could see nothing wrong with wanting Lenny to stay put.

"You think you can beat me?" He looked up at her. "You think if I used the same strength that Lenny has, you can take me down?"

"Are you serious?" She nodded and told him to stand. "You want me to knock the shit out of you? Then what? Have Ryland kill me?"

"No. I told him what we were going to do. You think that because you're a male and I'm a mere woman that you can protect me, right?" He thought there was a trap but nodded anyway. "Okay then, you try to knock me on my ass. I won't use any other strength than Lenny has in her current condition. Hurt."

"So you want me to fight you. You're fucking nuts. I'm not going to swing at you. You're a girl. And I can't hurt you." He took a step back when she took one toward him. "Seriously, Bronwyn, I'm not going to fight with you. So just get that stupid thought out of your head right now."

The punch nearly knocked him off his feet. When she swung at him again, he ducked and she got him in the belly. He took two steps back from her just as she came around with a roundhouse that did knock him down.

"I'm winning so far and I'm not even using the strength I know she has. You gonna just let me take you?" He stood up, pissed off now. "Come on, big bad Jules, show me what you got."

Chapter 8

Naomi wanted to scream, but she only stared at the wolf in front of her. She couldn't even kill him right now either. Without Milo there to help her, she hadn't fed yet and she was starving. The wolf had told her when he came in that if she fed from him she'd die because he'd taken precautions. She wasn't sure what they were, but she could smell the bite of silver around him and stayed in her chair.

"He was spotted hanging around the house until about six this morning. Then he left. I watched him go north on the main road, but I lost him after that. There was a great deal of activity at the house when I returned, but I didn't ever hear what had happened. Also...." He paused just enough that she leaned forward in her chair. "He's marking the place. I don't know if he realizes it or not yet, but the large wolf that is running the security team has found his marking and knows that they're not a part of his pack."

"I don't know a great deal about your kind. Tell me what you mean." Naomi knew very little about anything actually, because Milo had kept up with that part of her business. "I'm a little short staffed right now."

He didn't look to where the blood still stained the floor from her watcher. It was like acid to her and she couldn't clean it. Her mouth, too, was sore and she wasn't even sure whether the man had told her she could bite him. Smiling without revealing her teeth, she nodded for him to go on.

"Marking an area is nature to us. Every time we smell another wolf, we have the need to remark it. Lamb would have had the same needs. More so because he was once an alpha." She nodded, still no clue what he was talking about. Lamb had been an alpha? News to her.

"Will this head of security be able to find Lamb now? Will he know when he comes within a few feet of the place now?" The wolf—she had no idea what his name was, but had seen him talking to Milo before—nodded, then shook his head. "He will be able to find him or not?"

"Yes, mistress, he'll be able to find him, but more like miles from him instead of feet. He's an alpha, as I said, and his mark is stronger to keep away other males. The head of security will know him by scent now. He will be able to hunt him down as well."

More than she could do right now. He still wasn't answering her calls, and no matter how many times she left him messages to call her back, he wasn't doing it. And the worst part was she had no idea how to find him. She eyed the man in front of her, who started shaking his head.

"Even if I could find him, I wouldn't be able to give you the information. Not because I wouldn't want to, but because he'd kill me. He doesn't want to be found, and I'm sure that he'd be really be pissed off at me even if I could find him. Which I probably couldn't. He's that good." He handed her a Baggie. "This is what his scent is.

It's not as good as a piece of his clothing or fur, but he marked those leaves and his scent is on them."

She took them, wondering what the hell she was supposed to do with this, and it occurred to her he was telling her if she wanted the wolf then she had to find him herself. She looked over at the stain again. Milo would have found him for her.

"I suppose if I asked you to keep looking for him for me, you'd not do that either. You're just too afraid. I'm thinking I have very little use for you, wolf, if you can't carry out a few minor details that I need." He shrugged and she wanted to come across the desk and strangle him. "You do know that there are other ways to kill you other than biting you, don't you?"

He stood up and shifted. Just like that, the man was gone and the wolf, huge and his teeth snapping at her, made her lean back as far as she could from him. He snarled at her, then crashed through the window just behind him, and took off to the woods.

"Fucking bastard. As if I don't have enough shit in this room to replace." She looked around the room that had been cleared of the all the debris and wondered how the fuck she was supposed to get the things back to normal in there. She couldn't shop during the day, of course, and her computer had taken a lot of the damage she'd created. Naomi tried to decide if she could call the local computer store, and realized that there would be no one awake when it arrived. She simply had to find her a watcher, but those were so hard to find nowadays, too. She simply didn't know where to turn.

When she looked back at the broken window, she saw one of those fucking vampires lurking around her yard. Taking them into her fold had been the stupidest thing she'd ever done. She told him to come in, and he sat in the chair across from her. She could smell the blood all over him immediately.

"What have you been up to?" He grinned at her, his teeth a nasty stained black. "You do know that you can use a toothbrush still, right? I mean, your breath must about kill your prey when you lean over to drink from them."

"I'm menacing." She rolled her eyes. "I wanted to tell you what we've done just so when you see it on the news, you'll know we did it. We killed another family like before."

"Why?" He shrugged, and she took a deep breath and counted to ten. "Okay, why did you feel the need to let me know when I couldn't care one shit what you do so long as it doesn't come back to bite me in the ass?"

"You said that girl that killed Ben was a detective and that she was retired." She remembered something like that, but right now she was more focused on finding her and killing her than anything else.

"So? You're killing and she is no longer even on the case. What did you hope they'd do, call her back in for help? Not fucking likely. They think she was the one who killed that cop. And that was a major fuck up on your part, too. What the hell were you thinking calling that in? Do you have any idea how many minds we had to erase? We finally just gave up and started killing them."

"They would have to go in and arrest her for another death, right?" She wanted to snap his neck. There could be no way he was this stupid.

"Arrest her for deaths that she couldn't have committed because she'd been in another state? Or the fact that she's been sliced up so badly she can hardly walk?"

She shook her head. "They'd be lucky if she could get to the jail without hurting herself. What I'd really like to know is why the fuck you haven't brought her to me?"

"You want us to bring her to you?" She stood up, tempted to kill him where he sat. "You said we was to find her. You never said we was to bring her to you. Hell, we could have done that weeks ago."

She had him against the far wall before she could think about what she should or shouldn't do. When he struggled for air, she thought about telling the moron he didn't need air, but liked the feeling of him trying to fight her. She banged his head against the wall hard enough that she smelled blood erupt from him.

"You'll find her tonight and bring her back here or so help me, I'll kill you all." He nodded at her, his eyes as wide as saucers. "And she will be unharmed so that I can do it. Do you understand me?"

He nodded, and she dropped him. "Mistress, we was—" She held up her hand as she walked to the desk. Whatever he had to say was going to get him ended right now and she needed him. When she sat down, she told him to get out.

It took her almost an hour to calm down. By that time she'd made her a list, two actually, and had discarded most of the things on them. But the few that remained were a good start.

Find a watcher. She knew that the Holders of the Realm would help vampires when their watcher had been killed, but she was pretty sure that they'd stake her out in the sun if she went to them for help. She'd just have to find one on her own. She'd start with someone from the nearby town. Surely one of them would help out a vampire for enough money.

Second on her list was to find out what Viktor knew. She hated the man for what he'd put her through, but she was more afraid of him than anything. And if he found out that the kid she was trying to kill was her daughter, she was afraid he'd do something horrific to her and she'd beg him for death.

The third thing on her list was forgotten as she remembered the first time she'd met the man. He'd been so handsome and slick that she'd wanted to drop her vampire and go and work for him. He had so many rules that she'd given up on the idea even before she'd gone to him, but he had approached her not long after her daughter was born.

"You're going to murder your own child if you do not get some help with her. She is too precious to leave to starve for so many days." Naomi had glanced at the child in the crib and shrugged. "Will you consider giving her to another for safe keeping?"

"Her? I could care less what happens to her, but Grunt liked her well enough." He did seem to like her, but Naomi had other things on her mind. "When will you release Grunt from the prison? It has been several months, and I need him with me."

Viktor had shaken his head. "It has been only a few days, and you will see him soon enough. I must insist that you feed the child. She is dying; are you aware of that?"

Naomi was but didn't really care. She picked up the baby and shook her a little, and heard Viktor's sharp intake of breath. She turned to look at him, confused about why he should care so much. She wondered if he wanted her for himself, but knew that couldn't be right. Viktor had Peter, and everyone knew the men were gay.

"We are not lovers." He took the baby from her, cut open his wrist, and pressed it to her lips. "You will do well to keep her safe from now on, Naomi. She will have my blood now, and I will come hunting for you should she be harmed again. What is it you've called her?"

Called her? If the child had a name at all, she had no idea what it was. When she'd gotten pregnant with her all those months ago, she'd only kept the child because Grunt had wanted her to. Now that he wasn't there to take care of it, she found she hated it even more than when it was misshaping her body. She watched as the brat suckled from his wrist.

"You can have her." She smiled at his surprised look. "I don't want her, and I'll give her to you if you release Grunt to me now. Otherwise she might not survive the next time I take her out in the car."

"You'd trade your child for that monster." It wasn't a question, but she nodded anyway. "You do know that she will have powers you won't. She'll be stronger than you will ever be. And she'll hate you for this."

"Like I care. Give me Grunt and I'll be happy. She can be the next leader of all vampires for all I care. I just want my lover back." He sealed the wounds at his wrist, snapped his fingers, and the brat was gone. "We have a deal then?"

"We do. But I will take something from you at her maturity. When she reaches her age, I will come and take all that you have from you." She tried to focus on what he was saying to her, but all she could think about was no brat and her Grunt was coming home. "Do you understand what I am telling you, Naomi? You'll have nothing."

"Yeah, yeah. Give me Grunt or bring back the kid." And he had done what he'd told her. Grunt and she had gone on a feeding spree that had lasted for a week. Then he'd asked her about the kid and she lied to him. She told him that she'd died.

And now in four days, her kid was going to turn twenty-five—the age of her majority. She had to kill her before then or she'd lose it all. Everything she'd worked so hard for.

~~~

Lenny stepped into the kitchen to chaos. Jules was sitting at the table with an ice pack on his face, Ryland was laughing so hard tears streamed down his face, and the other four men in the room were having a hard time not laughing, too. She looked at her grandma.

"They had this bet, I guess. Bronwyn and this young man made a deal and he lost. I'm not entirely sure what the bet was about, because every time someone starts to tell me, they start laughing again." Grandma handed Jules the bottle that she had in her hand. "I think, from what I can gather, it was about you."

"Me? I didn't do anything." She looked at one of the men she didn't know when he coughed loudly. "What is it, buddy? You need something?"

"She was pissed at the way he's been treating you." Lenny glanced at Jules, who stiffened. "She said she wanted to see if he could knock her on her ass with her using the same strength you have being hurt."

"No, you're telling it wrong. She said she'd let him try. She damned near had him begging, too, before Ryland held her back." She looked at Ryland, who was wiping the tears away and nodding.

"She kicked his ass all over the yard and back. Didn't even get a chance to touch her." Ryland started laughing again and she smiled. It wasn't what he was saying that was funny, but the fact that he could hardly tell the story without laughing. Then Jules dropped the rag and stood up, and she got a good look at him and what had been done to him.

"Christ, what did she use? A bat?" He glared at her and she took a step back, then two forward. "If you think she hurt you, look at me like that again and I will tear you to pieces."

He must have believed her because he took a step back and shook himself until he was not so stiff. She looked over as all the men left the room, and Ryland and her grandma even took a hasty step back.

"Both of you have a seat." She looked at Ryland and stood still as he changed his tone a little. "Please have a seat. We're going to get this taken care of now or else."

"What taken care of?" When Ryland didn't answer her, she sat down. Jules had already sat down and she scooted her chair as far from him as she could. She looked at Ryland again, wondering if Jules wanted any more ice.

"You two are mates." She started to stand again and he barked at her to sit. "I'm not going to have this conversation again."

"I don't fucking care to hear it now. We might be mates of your kind, but not mine. I don't want nor do I need a babysitter, and I will never be a stay at home woman who rears the kiddies while the man of the house goes out and brings home the fucking bacon. I don't even like bacon."

Ryland glanced at Jules, then back at her. "You know that he's marked you? And because he didn't tell you, he is subject to being thrown from this streak."

She looked at Jules when he stood up. It wasn't really fair that he got to pace when she couldn't and started to say so to Ryland, when what he had said occurred to her. She glared at him.

"What do you mean 'thrown from the streak'? You mean you'd toss out your own brother because he did something without your permission? Or mine, for Christ's sake?" He nodded. "Why the fuck for? You think anyone gives a shit that he marked me? Do you think I do?"

"You don't care that I bit you?" She looked at Jules. "You're my mate, and it's my responsibility to make sure that no other male can—"

"Responsibility? I'm not your responsibility any more than I'm his." She pointed to the bird out the window feeding from the feeders. "And I'm a damned site more able to care for me than he is. Probably you, too. I'm not a child or a fool. And if you think either of those is true, then maybe you need another lesson today, this one from me."

Jules rolled his neck when Ryland laughed. He looked at her and glared. "I'm not in the habit of having someone needing me." She snorted.

"I got news for you...I don't want or need you. I have a job to do, and if you're going to be a pissy ass about it, I'd prefer that you'd stay the hell away from me. I have enough problems without you being another one."

"They hurt you." She nodded. "Let me see. Let me see what they did to you. All of you. Please?"

"Why? Why do you want to see me? That isn't going to change my mind about being your mate." She looked at

Ryland. "I was sliced up really badly, but I survived without a mate. I lived because of me, not who I am to someone else."

Ryland stood when she didn't move. Jules took a step back, and it took her a few seconds to realize that Ryland was pissed off, not at Jules but at her. When she lifted her chin at him, he smiled.

"You'll not take him as your mate because of this? You'd rather be alone than with him?" She nodded. "Then you leave me no choice. I have to banish him from the streak."

"Because of me?" He shrugged. "You fucking bastard. You can't do that to your own brother. Why the fuck did you come into my life? I never asked for any of this."

"No. I can see that. And I can also see that you'd rather have things your own way rather than see if you can work these things out. Well, I can't allow that." She started to ask him why not when he braced his arms over his chest and continued. "He's marked you, and even though you've not mated, you have bonded. So long as you are around him or him you, he'll go crazy with wanting to be with you. Even to the point of killing others if you were to take a lover."

As if to prove his point, Jules growled low at them both and took a step toward her. "She'll not be taking anyone but me to her bed."

"A lover. You think that someone would want to take me to their bed?" She laughed bitterly. "I'll be lucky if I can get a doctor to examine me without puking on me, much less a man wanting to fuck me." Jules growled again. "Oh, fucking grow up. This is what I look like."

She ripped open her shirt and tore the bandage off that she'd only just put on. She knew what that looked like because she'd had no choice but to see it. Stripping off her pants, she stood before them in her panties and bra, and when they both continued to look at her, she turned around to give them the full view.

"As I ran across the room, he sliced at me. I thought he was using a knife, something so sharp that the pain was there long after I felt my skin open. And by a long time I mean seconds instead of an instant. When I fell to the floor, he tore at my legs, running his claws down my calves to the bone through the muscles there. The doctor told me I had fallen against a fence or a fire grate, and that I wasn't cut at all but burned." She turned around as she finished. "Then when the vampire flipped me over, I watched my friend being held to another monster's mouth as he drank from him. When he was finished, he simply broke his neck. When I looked back at my body, he'd sliced my legs and arms. Tore them open like he was flaying a chicken breast from the bone. Even as I lay there bleeding from every part of my body, he told me that he wished he had more time to play. Wished that he had more of an art to killing like his master. That she had wanted me dead, but she said it was up to him how. Then he raked his claws across my belly, tearing it open until he—"

"That's enough. Please, no more." She glared at Ryland and shook her head at him. "Please no—"

"You wanted this story; well, you're fucking going to hear it. As he sliced open my belly, he pulled out my intestines and licked them, telling me that he was going to wrap them around my body like a dress and style my hair with my blood. He said that he'd done it before and loved the way the red streaked through it, liked how it felt to use such a warm gel to make me the most beautiful corpse he'd ever seen. I was going to be his masterpiece. Then I stabbed him in the eye and killed him." She picked up her shirt and held it in front of her, knowing it was too late to be modest now. "But I lived. I survived to be questioned daily by the police on what I had done to the man I was with. How I had managed to hurt myself so badly and kill an officer with nothing more than a knife. Where I had been when the supposed call had come in, and why would I tell everyone that I remembered nothing?" She looked at Jules when he spoke softly.

"I'm sorry. I'm sorrier than I've ever been in all of my life for what I've done to you." He looked at his brother. "I'll be out first thing in the morning. I'll...I'd like to say goodbye to the others."

"Yes, that's fine. And I'm sorry, Jules." He nodded at Ryland and left her standing in the kitchen with Ryland as he turned to speak to her. "I'm sorry as well, Lenny. You'll not need to have any more contact with us unless you want it."

Then he, too, was gone. Lenny picked up her pants and pulled them on, then went to her room and looked around. She was finished as well. She was just beginning to pack her things to go back to Washington when her grandma told her someone was there to see her. She went to the front of the house and saw two men standing there on the outside of the threshold. She knew them both.

"So, you've finally decided to show yourself." Viktor nodded, and Peter smiled. "Well too fucking bad. I'm finished with this little town and I'm going back to my old life."

She slammed the door in their faces and went back to packing. She was going to be gone before the sun set if she had to walk the entire way.

Chapter 9

"So you're going to just let her walk out of your life." Jules didn't turn to see his sister-in-law. He finished throwing the piece he'd been working on all day. He didn't bother answering Rayne. He'd learned from that mistake earlier today.

Rayne was a little blunter than Ally, who had just left, and a great deal scarier. Em had been mean in that she'd destroyed the two pieces that he'd had nearly finished. When Bronwyn had come in second, he'd thought he was prepared for about anything, but he'd been wrong. Very wrong. She was one pissed off female.

He set the piece aside before getting up to get another ball of clay to throw. Rayne was sitting on the only other chair in the room, and he had to walk around her twice to get what he needed. She finally stood up and blocked his way.

"I'm trying to work here." She looked around and smiled. "Please don't do that. I have a show in a few more weeks and these pieces are paid for by a very big name."

"Are you working to forget her, or do you even care what happens to her when she gets back to Washington?" Jules had thought of nothing else, but he doubted that she'd believe him. The others hadn't.

"She made her decision, and so have I. She'll be fine. Better probably than she would have been staying here." He moved to the wheel again. "She's a lot stronger than anyone ever gave her credit for."

Every time he blinked, he saw her body. Lush and full, scarred and marred, but simply the most beautiful thing he'd ever seen. She'd done more than survive. She'd gone against all odds and lived to tell about it, but she'd also done something more. She'd done what she had wanted, something even with all his money he had not been able to do for a long while.

He glanced at Rayne when she didn't say anything. "I talked to my agent this morning. I'm taking some time off and going to travel. I've…it's been a long time since I've done something for me, and I'm going to take the time to smell the roses, as cliché as that sounds."

"Why?" He shrugged at her question. "Don't give me that shit. What are you going to do and why? You never do anything without a plan that's been tweaked fifty times over and planned for months…where you're going and how long you're going to be gone, to the second."

"I'm going to have the studio redone and when I return, I'm going to make art for me, not for what I think someone will buy. I have enough money now that I can do what I please. And if they don't like it…." He didn't finish, and she didn't ask him to explain. "I don't have a clue how long I'll be gone, either."

She pulled the chair over to where he was working and sat in it so that he could see her if he looked up. She sat there for so long that he got into his zone and forgot she was there until he finished throwing. He looked at her briefly as he went to weigh up more clay balls.

"Ryland said you'd been asked to leave the streak." He didn't answer because it wasn't a question and even if it was, he didn't want to answer it. "He said that you didn't question it but seemed to welcome it."

He hadn't really, but he could see where Ryland would think that. He hadn't argued about him being able to stay, and knew for whatever reasons Ryland had, Jules had fucked up with Lenny and he deserved whatever came his way. As he centered the clay on the wheel, he looked up at Rayne.

"She's gone." She nodded, knowing, he supposed, who he was talking about. "I hurt her. Worse than the wounds she got, I cut her just as deeply by not trusting her. But mostly because I saw her as no one else ever would."

"Her wounds." Jules shook his head. "Ryland said you and him saw her body. That he was pretty sure that she'd never done that before. He said he'd have nightmares for years thinking about what she went through and endured."

"I was talking about her heart. I could have had it if I'd been less of a stubborn fool. I could have had it all but for being an idiot about what I wanted and what I was going to do for her." He laughed as he sat back with mud all over him. "I was going to take care of her. I was going to do things for her...I was going to make her mine and then put her away until I felt like I needed her to come out and be with me. I would have caged her."

"I doubt you would have done that to—"

"I would have. Not with an actual cage but with chains of restrictions. I didn't want a mate and was going to not have one unless it suited me and my timeframe."

He leaned into the clay again, centering it with his upper body. "I was a fool."

"You don't have to be." He looked up just as he was wetting the clay again to pull up the shape he wanted. "You can still be with her. I'm sure that if you went to her and told her what you told me, she'd take you back."

Jules pulled the clay up about two inches and then fanned it out to make the bowl in the middle. He thought about what Rayne said, but knew that he didn't want her out of pity; he wanted her because she wanted him.

"What the fuck are you waiting on, Jules?" He looked up at her, startled by her abrupt change. "You want her to get killed? She will, you know. She's not strong enough to go up against…. The evening she was hurt, did you know that Keith found the scene that she'd been working before she and her boss had gone to that house? That the computer system that he hacked at the station had all sorts of things on it, including pictures of the scene? That the things that vampire told her he was going to do to her were the same things that had been done to that family at the scene she'd been working?"

"She said she was working a crime scene, and that's all. She never said she remembered that." Rayne shook her head. "What do you know? And how do you know it was the same scene?"

"There were several dead bodies in the house. A mother, father, infant boy, and an older son and daughter, all of whom were killed that day. The killers had gutted them, all but the baby. Brock said he was also able to pull some records and found that the baby had had its neck broken. The mother had had her hair styled with her blood, and she'd been dressed in her guts." Rayne started to pace. "The little girl, too, but the boy simply had his throat cut open. But the man…they'd taken their time with him. They had sliced open his legs and arms and then they…."

He waited, not sure if he wanted to hear or not, but when she turned to him, Jules knew as surely as he was sitting there he didn't want to know. But he had to. He had to know to better understand the horror that Lenny had gone through.

"His fingers were cut off, as well as his toes. His dick and balls, too. Then the sick fuck spread them out on the floor in sort of a morbid kind of art. Adding his tongue and eyes to where his head might have been with the other body parts." She turned to him. "She saw that. Cataloged it all down on a notebook that was found at the scene by the new owners. Do you know what they said when Em asked them for it? They told her that they could no longer live in their home because of what had been written there. And when Brock went back the next week to speak to them again, they were gone. Not even bothering to take their furniture or clothes."

He stood up and washed his hands, leaving the piece he'd been working on not even half finished. As he dried his hands, he looked at Rayne. She wasn't smiling but looked as murderous as he'd ever seen her.

"Where is she?" She crossed her arms over her chest like he'd seen her do a million times when dealing with a stupid customer at her shop. "I need to help her if she'll let me, but I can't do anything if I don't know where to find her."

"She's not going to be happy with me." He didn't say he didn't care because he really did. "When you find her, what are you going to do first? If you say anything about taking care of her, I'm going to brain you."

"I'm going to ask her if I can be a part of her life. I'm going to beg her to give me a second, third, hell as many chances as I can get from her to show her how sorry I am and how much I admire her. I'm going to get down on my hands and knees to beg her to let me start over." Rayne smiled at him. "I'm going to see if she'll let me be her mate. Ask her to care for me and save me from my foolish self."

"That's a lot to ask a girl on the first round. Perhaps you should just ask her to forgive you and be done with it." She laughed when he shook his head. "So it's going to be all or nothing with you, huh?"

"It's the only way I can make sure she ever trusts me again." She nodded at him. "Will you help me?"

"She's at your mom's house. She's supposed to be stalling her until you get your act together and go over there and do what you should have done weeks ago…be a man." He kissed her on the cheek, and then for spite hugged her to him tightly, knowing that his brother wasn't going to like her smelling like another male.

"I'm going to find my mate and see if she'll have me." With that he picked up his keys and left the building. He hoped that Rayne would lock up but really didn't care. In a few weeks it would all be gone anyway if Lenny wouldn't take him back.

~~~

Sandra was running out of ideas to keep her there. This last attempt at stalling was bordering on insane. Who cared what the back end of her pool house looked like? If asked, Sandra would be hard pressed to tell anyone what she'd even said about it. She looked up when Lenny cleared her throat.

"You did really well until this." She tried to act like she didn't have any idea what she was talking about, but it wasn't working if Lenny's face was any indication. "Who talked you into this harebrained scheme? Ryland or Bronwyn?"

"All of them, as a matter of fact." She nodded toward the pool to have a chair. "I thought he'd come to his senses and come here for you. I guess I don't know my son as well as I thought."

"Perhaps it's me, not him. I didn't exactly make it easy on him to want me." Sandra doubted that. "I'm sort of a bitch on my worst days, and a fucking bitch on the days when I'm not. I'm not really rich people's kind of girl next door. I'm more of a beer in one hand and a gun in the other kind of girl. And usually pointing the gun at the man who's trying to feel me up."

"Jules didn't try to feel you up?" The words spilled from her mouth before she could think them out. "Good heavens, that didn't come out right. What I meant was that I can't believe that other men would.... Well shit, Lenny, that's exactly what I meant. He's been somewhat of a loner most of his life, and his first date was a set up made by one of his brothers. I suppose he had a good time...Jules, not his brother. Brock could and did have fun no matter what he was doing. Keith will continue to have no fun unless there's something electrical in front of him. The others have settled down, but I do worry over them. All of them. But Jules, he's the one that I worried about the most."

"There's nothing wrong with any of your sons, Sandra. They are all very...manly." Sandra burst out laughing. "I didn't mean that the way it sounded either."

"Yes you did, and you know it." Sandra laughed again. "They are good boys, the best I would have to say, but they do love their mates. Keith will be next, I suppose, but I'm almost afraid to see what she'll be like. The women are getting stronger as they each find their mates."

"I'm not his mate. He'll find someone else. He'll be much happier with someone else." Sandra saw Jules striding toward them and had to smile. "What happens now will be better for all of you."

"I highly doubt that." Sandra stood up when Jules spoke. He didn't sound any happier than she'd been with Ryland when he'd told her what he'd done to his brother. "Mother, I'd like a word in private with Lenny, please."

"I have nothing to say to you. What are you doing here anyway? Shouldn't you be off sulking somewhere about how I wouldn't mind you? If you want to start listing all the things I did wrong, then you are going to have to toss the fucking thing away. I don't want to hear them. I've had enough of you, thanks."

"I love you." Lenny sat down, and so did Sandra. That she hadn't expected. Before she could move out of the chair to leave, Jules continued. "I've been a fool. A major one at that. I only wanted what I wanted, and didn't care about or even concern myself with what your needs or wants were."

"If you're hoping to get an argument from me, you are waiting in vain. I think that you might have left out a few descriptive words I would have used to describe you. You forgot 'bossy' and 'pig-headed.' Then there's 'jackass' and 'know-it-all'. Oh, and let's not forget—"

The kiss shut her up. Sandra watched them for several seconds before she thought to leave. As she moved out of the backyard and into the house, she tried to think who to call first. Rayne had set this whole thing up, but Keith had found out all the information when no one else had. Sandra thought of calling Ryland, too, to ask him to reinstate his brother's name in the streak, but then she wondered if that, too, had been a ploy. It seemed her family was playing matchmaker better than she was. She sat down at the table and nearly screamed when Peter and Viktor were suddenly in front of her.

"We have to speak to them." She shook her head and told Viktor that now was not a good time. "But the vampires mean to kill her soon, and we know some information that Lenore will need to know."

"If you tell them about it tonight or tomorrow, will it make that much difference? I mean, they're going to need time to come together. They need each other. Can't you just...I don't know, protect them tonight so they can become a couple?"

Peter went to the window and looked out. She couldn't see around either man as they stood there blocking her view, but she knew when they turned, it had been just what she'd hoped for.

"They are in the pool house." Peter smiled. "We can't protect them, but we can make sure to stay close. In the event that anyone comes here, we can warn them."

Sandra nodded, then looked at Viktor when he cleared his throat. "You should call your family together for tomorrow during the day. We have much to share with them. Some of the information is...some of it we've only just discovered ourselves."

"I can do that. How about one o'clock tomorrow? I'll have them all here and we can figure this out together. They will be...I'm hoping that they will have worked out their differences by then, and are well on their way to becoming a couple."

Peter laughed. "I don't believe there is any doubt on that, my lady. I believe our young Jules will be a better man for what he's going to get out of having her as a mate."

Viktor nodded. "Her birthday is the day after tomorrow. She will be in the most danger between now and then. If she dies, all is lost."

"Lost how? Will Jules and she be able to survive this?" Viktor shrugged at her. "Well that's no answer, is it? I demand that you tell me what's going on now. You've been keeping your secrets about this girl long enough. What is it about her that has you so...you're afraid for her? Good heavens, you're her father, aren't you?"

"No, my lady, I'm not. But I did have a hand in keeping her safe when she was but an infant. I wish she was my child. I could save her from the monster that comes for her. I could simply give her my powers and let her take out the one that would have her dead before her date of birth."

Sandra sat down and tried to think what was going to happen and how she was going to be able to save her family. Not just her sons but their wives and children as well. She wanted them all to be safe. She glanced at the back door and hoped that Jules and Lenny would have a long life together, but the look on the two vampires' faces was not making her feel very positive about their future.

"Will she die if this person gets her?" Neither man answered her. Sandra felt the weight of this bear down on her. "Well, can you tell me, does she have a chance at coming out on top?"

"More than she would have without a mate." Sandra nodded. "My lady, she is only as strong as she wishes to be. And with her mate beside her, she can be invincible."

Sandra didn't believe anyone was invincible and told them so. "Every person has a weakness. Every being, including the two of you. But they can be as strong as they could be and come out the winners because of it. Jules told her he loved her. I believe him. I also believe in love, and the fact that it can make everything work out. So you tell me who this person is that is trying to harm them, and I'll see what I can do about getting enough back up here should they need it.

"Her mother."

Chapter 10

Jules locked the door to the pool house. She'd agreed to come in here so they could have some privacy, but he hoped that they wouldn't be leaving until tomorrow morning, if not the late afternoon. She turned to look at him when he moved to the center of the room and turned on the fireplace to take the chill off the room.

"What do you mean, you love me? Why? How did that happen all of the sudden?" She started pacing as he moved to one of the couches that surrounded the fireplace and stood near it. "You just want to get back in with your family and you'll say anything to me to make it happen. Well, it won't work."

"I never thought it would and that's not why I said it to you. I do love you. But like any idiot, it took me a while to figure it out." He sat on the couch and watched her move back and forth. "I was wrong about everything. But not about loving you."

"Do I have to take off my clothes again to show you what I look like?" The thought of her taking off her clothes had him pulling a pillow over his lap. "You did see what that monster did to me, didn't you? How he left me there to die?"

"Yes. And when you showed me, all I could think about was how much you had suffered and how lovely you looked." She started to speak, but he cut her off. "You are the most beautiful creature I've ever had the pleasure of seeing. Your skin is soft and warm. Your breasts...when I tasted them through the sheet, it was all I could do not roar out that you were mine."

"I'm not whole." He moved to the edge of the couch and crawled on his knees to her. He was afraid she'd bolt, but she stood still as he wrapped his arms around her thighs and laid his head on her abdomen.

"To me, Lenny, you're more than whole. You're everything to me." He held her this way until he felt her fingers in his hair. When she tightened in it, he looked up at her. "I want you. I want your heart and your body. I want to show you how much you mean to me, how much you'll always mean to me."

"Why?" He kissed her hip, then her belly. He opened her pants and pulled them off her slowly, as reverently as he could without hurting her. She stepped out of one leg, then the other, and he ran a hand down each pinked place where she'd been stitched back together.

"When we're hurt as cats, we can shift and we're as good as new. Even in reverse we can shift to cats to care for our human self. Had I known you before this, I would have changed you into a tiger and you would never have these reminders." He looked up at her. "That's all they are, Lenny, reminders. They don't define you. They have made you stronger, but they didn't make you. You did that all by yourself."

Jules kissed the area right above her panty line and inhaled. She smelled like heaven and he wanted to taste it. Moving his hands up her body slowly, he slid his hands under her shirt and up to her belly, where the bandage had not been replaced. He lifted the shirt up, and she pulled it off and dropped it to the floor. When she put her hands over her wounds, he pulled them away.

"Never with me, love. Never hide yourself from me." He kissed the one closest to her hip and licked his tongue along it. "I can heal you this way. Not internally, but these wounds."

She moaned when he flicked his tongue over her navel and he suckled the crevice into his mouth and nipped. She rocked her hips toward him and he cupped her ass cheeks and brought her closer to him.

"Jules, please. I can't stand up any longer." He grinned. "Please, just let me lie down on the couch or something."

"I would rather taste you like this." He slid his finger down her ass and to her opening and found her to be wet and hot. "You will let me drink from you like this, won't you, Lenny? You'll let me suck on your pretty clit until you come, and then allow me to drink deeply from you?"

She moaned his name again, and he took that as her assertion and tore her panties from her and buried his mouth over her. Christ, she was going to make him come from just tasting her. Spreading her thighs wider for him, he drank from her and knew that even if he had his whole life, he'd never tire of her. Sliding his finger into her sheath, he felt her juices run down his hand and to his elbow. He couldn't drink from her fast enough.

When her knees started to tremble, he lifted his head and looked up at her. She swayed and he stood up and lifted her into his arms. He took her to the bedroom that he knew was in the pool house and laid her on the bed. She looked up at him with lust-glazed eyes.

"I'm going to make love to you." She nodded. "All night and every night for the rest of our lives, if you'll have me."

"You want me? Even after this?" She put her hands over her belly and he dropped to his knees beside the bed and moved her hands. "I'm not like other women."

"No, you're not. Thank God. You're lovelier than any other woman I've met." He kissed her navel again, glad to find such an erotic place on her body. "You're stronger than me, smarter, and a great deal more patients as well. I would have shot me long ago."

"You do make a good case for carrying a gun." He tried to look wounded but made her laugh. "Are you really going to sleep with me?"

He shook his head and smiled when she looked disappointed. "I'm thinking we aren't going to get a great deal of sleep. Will it make you mad if I bit you again, marked you?"

"No. I think...will your tiger bite me as well?" His cat stirred along his skin, and he purred. "I can see him in you. When you're angry or...sexually aroused, I can see him."

Jules let a little of his cat go and felt his skin crawl with fur before changing back to human flesh. When she ran her fingers over his throat, he moaned. And when she lifted her head and licked the area there, he cupped the back of her head and held her there.

"Bite me, love. Mark me with your bite." Her teeth grazed along his skin, and he felt his cat snarl at her to do it. When her teeth grazed his skin, he growled low and she lifted her head.

"Will it hurt?" He shook his head, unable to say anything just now. "If I bite you, will you be mine?"

"Yes," he hissed at her and brought her back to his neck. "Do it, Lenny. Mark me as your mate and taste my blood."

When her teeth broke skin, he lifted her hair out of the way and bit her shoulder as well. He reached between her legs and pinched her clit hard, and she screamed around his shoulder. Every part of him wanted to flip her over to her belly and take her hard, but he had to be careful yet of her wounds. When she lifted her head, he felt his cat snarl and he had to fight to hold him in check.

"Let him go. I want to see him." She was panting hard, and he wanted her more than ever. "Give me to him, Jules. I want to have him mark me."

He let him go. Even as he took him, Jules knew that he wanted more than to simply bite her and mark her. He wanted her. Jules looked at her through his cat's eyes and purred low. She lay back on the bed and he joined her there.

Her belly was bleeding a little, and his cat leaned down and swiped his tongue over the wounds. They would heal quicker now and not be as sore. When he nosed her pussy, Jules tried to call him back, but Lenny moaned. When she opened her legs for him, his cat moved in to taste her.

His tongue was wider and thicker than Jules's, but he didn't enter her. He only tasted her once before moving up to her throat. Jules's breath caught when she tilted her head for the big cat, and when he sank his teeth deep into her muscle, he knew that he wasn't just marking her; he was claiming her as well. Even as his teeth marred her lovely skin, Jules brought his cat back and lifted his head from her shoulder.

"I need to be inside of you. Now, love. To complete our bond, I have to come with you as we bite. Can we...will you be mine, please?" She nodded, and he shook his head. "You have to say it, baby. I know that we've already surpassed this part, but I need to hear you say that you're mine."

"I'm yours. I need you, please. I'm all yours." Jules settled between her legs and moved so that his cock was just at her entrance. She moaned and rolled her hips, and he felt his tip slide into her and he moaned. "Please? I need you."

Taking her mouth with his, he moved deep into her. He wanted to go slow, enjoy her, but she was so hot, so tight that he had to have more of her. When he moved his mouth to her breasts, she arched up and fed him. Her nipples tasted so delicious that he wanted to bite. Cupping them in his palm, he lifted her ass up so that he could fill her. When she wrapped her legs around his thighs, he knew that he was going to come soon.

"When you come, you need to bite me again." She moaned. "Lenny, love, I'm so close. Do you understand me?"

"Yes. Oh please, I'm coming." Her body bowed up and then she shattered. He watched her come apart and then together again before he remembered he needed to claim her. As soon as he licked the area at her shoulder, he felt her do the same. Once they did this, there was no turning back. When she screamed out another powerful climax, he sank his canines into her shoulder and felt her bite him as well. The immediate and profound connection took his breath away.

Come again. Now, Lenny, come again. She lifted her head from him and screamed before he could let his own body have a release. He suckled as much of her into him again and sank his teeth deeper. With a hard shake of his head to mark her for all to see, he let go and roared out his release against her skin.

~~~

Naomi woke from her sleep and sat up in the dark room. Something had happened. She had no idea what it was but could feel…something wasn't right. She lay back down and tried to rest, but whatever had waked her was still there. When she rolled to her side and tried to concentrate on the feeling, all she got for her troubles was a feeling of emptiness and something akin to terror.

Sitting up again, she moved to the blackened window and put her hand on the glass. It was only about four o'clock; still hours before she should have been waked. Moving to the bathroom, she switched on the light and looked at herself.

Her mouth was still sore, but she could at least feed now. Of course, she had to cut the vein open when she did it, but she didn't really care so long as she could eat. She should have known better than to kill her watcher, no matter how badly he'd pissed her off. She turned off the light and went to bed. Closing her eyes, she had a feeling that whatever had woke her wasn't going to be anything she could solve until the sun went down, and she let sleep take her. Before she was fully asleep, she sat up in bed again.

She'd mated.

"Fuck." Naomi got up and started pacing the room. She had taken a mate, which meant that her daughter was going to get some of her powers with that. And even if she had some of the weaker ones her father had given her, it would be enough to defeat the vampires who had been trying to kill her, not to mention enough to knock her on her ass when and if she had to end up dealing with her on her own.

Naomi didn't want to have to deal with her at all, but knew that she was going to have to. And she just knew that Viktor had managed this because she didn't want a kid. And now she had to deal with this, and her Grunt was not even around to reap what they'd sown together in creating that brat.

"Now what the fuck am I supposed to do?" She didn't have any answers. But she knew one thing; she had to double her efforts to kill the brat. And if that failed, she would have to figure out a way to make nice with her so that she'd get her to beg her benefactor to let her mommy keep her powers.

Not likely, she thought. Her daughter had probably been told all sorts of stories about her since Viktor had taken her from her. Naomi smiled and wondered what the Realm would say if they thought that their precious Viktor and Peter had taken her little girl practically from her arms at birth and had never let her see her again.

Naomi felt a little puke back up in her throat on that thought. She couldn't even remember when she'd been taken away, only that she'd gotten her Grunt back. And as far as what she looked like, there was no way she would ever be able to tell them that. Not that her daughter had been much to look at. She'd been as bald as her father had been, and what little fuzz there was, it was that fucking red of his ancestors. And those eyes…dark green like the fields, he'd told her.

And now the bitch had a mate. She wondered what but didn't really care. She just hoped it wasn't one of the tigers. All she wanted to know was how to kill her before the clock struck midnight tomorrow night. She looked at the clock again and realized how little time she had left. Just over thirty hours left until she'd lose it all.

Naomi thought of Viktor. He'd visited her twice since he'd taken her daughter away. She'd been going by the name of Divinity the first time she'd seen him, and had never corrected him when he'd come back the next two times. The third and final time they'd met, she'd called him to her. She needed…a favor.

"Save him." She looked up at him from the body of her lover. "He's all I have. You have to save him for me. You owe me."

"Owe you? Whatever for?" She looked up at him, her mind scrambling to think of anything at all to make him save Grunt.

"I gave you my kid." He snorted, and she stood up, covered in Grunts's blood from the knife wound she'd given him when he'd pissed her off. "I did and now you owe me. You must save him for me or I'll…I'll—"

"You'll what, Divinity? Take her back? I think not. She is living well and awaiting her twenty-fifth birthday." He laughed and her skin crawled at the sound. "You do remember our deal, don't you? I take her and you lose it all when she matures. Do you have any idea what awaits you when that happens?"

"You said I'd lose all my powers. How can you do that to me? I've never done anything wrong to you other than a few things. Certainly not enough to make you take everything from me." She stepped over Grunt and to the man who had the power to harm her. "Please reconsider that demand. What is to become of me if you do that?"

"Not me, Divinity, but your daughter. It's her birthright. You'll give them to her and I can only imagine what goodness she will do with them. Then you will become human again." She had a moment of panic. Then she looked at him again.

"She was sickly when you took her. Maybe she won't live that long." She hadn't had any idea how long it had been since she'd handed her over, but it couldn't have been that long. "You said yourself that I was a bad parent on more than one occasion."

"You are a bad parent. But she is well. No reason for you to concern yourself with her dying before she can take her gift from you." She looked at him closely as he continued. "She will live and you will be human."

She took a step back and nearly tripped over Grunt. She'd forgotten about him and wondered how she was supposed to survive without him at her side. But when she turned back to ask—no, beg—Viktor to give her this last thing, he was gone. And so was Grunt a few seconds later, becoming nothing but ash.

Sitting in the dark stain, she ran her fingers through what was left of Milo and thought about being a human again. She knew that she'd not be able to survive as one again. It had been so long since she'd thought of herself as anything but a vampire, and longer still since she'd even been a human. She would not survive and knew it even back then. She had to do something. And that was when she came up with the plan to kill her daughter before that date.

It had taken her nearly ten years to hunt her down. Ten years of searching and waiting to see if it was really her. Milo, of course, had done most of the work, killing off children after finding them for her. Then she'd realize that she was still there, a small, yet constant reminder that her life was going to change.

She reached for the vampire who had informed her about Lamb and found him easily enough. She thought about summoning him to her, but decided to see what sort of riches her daughter was living in. But first she needed to feed and feed well. There was no reason to take the chance that there might be an encounter with her daughter, and doing so in a weakened state was just stupid.

Finding her prey took longer than she'd hoped, and it was closer to sunrise than she'd hoped when she got back to the house. Once she opened the vein, drinking from him made her slightly ill. She hated to drink from drug addicts and worst yet, ones that had been so riddled with all sorts of diseases that she had to work to filter them out of her system. So instead of leaving him with an open wound, she snapped his neck and left him to die. She had things to do. Arriving at the point where the vampire was nearly made her laugh.

He was treed. There was no other term for what was going on. Two wolves had him in a tree and were snapping at his feet. She watched as the fool tried to reason with them, beg them to let him pass freely. She wondered if he realized that he could simply disappear. Then she remembered just how young he was. He probably had no idea of what he could do even as a newborn.

"Kill them." He looked up at her in her perch higher in the tree than him, and she could see the confusion on his face. "Just kill them and be done with it. You do know how, don't you?"

"No." He looked back at the barking wolves, then at her. "Couldn't you just do it? I really would be happy to get out of this tree."

The sudden shot sounded and had both wolves running for cover as the vampire below her rained as ash to the ground. She looked at the man who came toward the tree she was in and knew immediately he was the wolf she'd been trying to contact for days now. She landed in front of him and grabbed him around the throat.

"You've been avoiding me." He didn't struggle but let her hold him. "What the fuck am I paying you for if you're going to kill my children and not the one I sent you to kill for me?"

"She's not here and he was drawing unwanted attention to you." She hadn't thought of that and looked around. "The girl hasn't been here for two days. All her things are packed up, and the old woman who watched over her is gone, too. I've been waiting to see if she returned today, but as she hasn't, I was going to the tiger's lair where she's been known to be."

Naomi dropped him and walked to the house. She could smell the cats around and several humans. There was even the strong smell of bear and panther. What the fuck was she doing here, running a fucking zoo?

"She's mated to someone as of last night. Is there one of the weres here that she could be especially close to?" He shrugged. "What do you know? What am I paying you for if you're not doing what I need?"

"She's not stupid. Smartest person I've ever come across in my work, as a matter of fact. You should have told me she has some training in that regard. She carries a gun loaded with silver, works out three times a day even if she is hurting. I've seen her fight, too. It was with a dummy, but she didn't have any trouble breaking it to shit when she needed to. And her knife throwing ability is amazing. She can hit dead center every time." He leaned against the wall where they were standing. "She's very beautiful, too. Flaming red hair, green eyes, and a complexion that could only be referred to as milky. I almost don't want to slit her throat."

"But you will and before midnight tomorrow night." He nodded. "Then what are you waiting for?"

"You." She looked at him, confused by what he meant. "I need more money. You've said I'd get payment when the job is done, but I want it now. She's as good as dead by the time you're having sleepy time and when it's done, I'm out of here. She has beings around her that...well, frankly, scare the shit out of me. And a vampire that is as old as I've ever felt."

She knew it could only be Viktor. "I don't carry that kind of money on me. You'll have to wait, and the sun is rising now in the event you haven't noticed. Come to me when the sun is going down and I'll have it."

He nodded and she disappeared. She was standing in her lair a few seconds later. She didn't have any money. She'd never found any use for it, and Milo again had taken care of whatever she needed to purchase. She was beginning to think he was more of a problem than she'd thought. She went to her bed to lie down. Things were not progressing in the direction she wanted them to. And she was going to have to step in if she didn't want the wolf to kill her after the daughter.

Chapter 11

The shower felt good on her abused body. Smiling, she thought the word abused wasn't quite right. She was sore from a night of sex and more sex. Jules was surprisingly strong when he needed to be. And very thorough. She doubted very much if there was a part of her body he'd not touched, kissed, or licked last night and through the night.

The shower door sliding on its tracks was all the warning she got before he was suddenly there.

"Why didn't you wait for me?" He wrapped his hands around her waist, and she turned to look at him. "I thought we'd shower together. I would love to wash your back if you'd wash mine."

"I thought you said you had to work this morning." He nodded as he kissed her throat. "And you said you had to pack up some things to be shipped out today for a show."

"I do, I did. I called the studio, and as we speak, it's being taken care of. I have to go in later to finish the things I started last night, but other than that...." He nipped at her pulse, which tripled in speed the moment he touched her. "Have I told you how much I love your taste?"

"Yes. Several times. We'll never get out of here if we take a shower together." He grinned as he moved his mouth to her breasts. "We really don't have any time for you to be doing this. Your mom said that we had to be at her house at twelve-thirty. It's almost eleven now."

"Plenty of time to do what I need to you." He was down on his knee before she realized he'd sat her on the little bench in the stall. She'd been thinking that it would be a wonderful way to shave your legs, and what he was doing now had her thinking she'd like one in every bathroom she entered.

He pulled her to the edge and spread her legs wide. She felt so exposed and tried to squeeze them closed when he shook his head. She watched as he moved his fingers up her leg to her pussy and then slipped them inside of her, and she nearly came up off the seat.

"You're so tight. I love watching your face when you're enjoying yourself. Every time I hit you in that perfect bundle of nerves," he said, touching them, "you light up like a Christmas tree and have me wanting to make you twinkle."

"Please." He leaned down and took her clit into his mouth and sucked hard. She leaned back further and moaned. "More. I need more of you."

"I want to drink from you until you fill me. Then I want to stand you against the tile and enter you. Would you like me to take you like that? Fuck you hard while you're wrapped around me?" She hissed out her answer, and he grinned. "Good. Don't hold back. We're on a time limit."

Before she could tell him she was already close, he nipped at her. She felt his tongue join his finger, and when he touched her nerve again and again, she knew she was going to come. He lifted her legs and put them over his shoulders, then she cried out and came apart when he pressed through the tight muscles at her ass.

That's it, baby. Come hard for me again. She was surprised to find him in her head and tried to touch him. *Think of me. You'll find the link.*

It was hard not to think of him when he was doing such delicious things to her body. And when he filled her more with another finger, she grabbed his head and held on as a climax took her. She was nearly on top of another one when he lifted his head and picked her up. She was over his cock and against the wall before she could take a breath. He kissed her as he slammed her over and over against the wall with his body.

"Come." She moaned when he barked at her. "Come for me and let me bite you. I want to feel your body come around mine while I mark you again."

She held him tightly to her and screamed loudly without holding back. As soon as he bit her, she came again, rolling on top of the second climax before the first one was finished. When he rocked incredibly harder into her, she bit the first thing she could touch with her mouth and soared over the top yet again. She couldn't hold on and let the darkness take her away.

Lenny woke in the bed. She looked around and realized she was alone. Smiling, she rolled to her side, pulled his pillow to her, and inhaled him. She was just putting it back when she heard a noise and looked up as he came out of the bathroom, smiling.

"You killed me." He lay down next to her as she continued. "I don't think a person is supposed to come that hard or that many times, do you?"

"Only if it's done correctly." He kissed her mouth quickly. "But we have to move. Your little nap is going to make us late. It's a little after twelve-thirty now."

She jumped out of bed only to freeze. The mirror in front of her was a full-length one, and she could see her entire body. Lenny turned and looked at Jules. He hadn't moved and she was sure he'd noticed what she was seeing, and not for the first time.

"When he licked the wounds, he gave you more of him than I thought." She looked back at the reflection and touched her smooth skin. "Your legs are better as well. I'm not sure why the scarring is gone, but the ones on your back are almost gone as well."

"It looks like nothing ever happened to me. And it doesn't hurt either." She looked at him in the mirror. "Did he do this to help me, or did you do it?"

"I didn't. I know it's hard to understand, but the tiger has a mind of his own. I can control him, but not entirely. He's a different being altogether. We're all like that with the exception of Brock. He can control his cat like me, but he has a second cat, one he calls his beast. He's actually bigger than his cat and much harder to control. Most of the time he can't." Jules sat up on the edge of the bed. "About last night when he licked your pussy...I didn't know he was going to do that, either. I didn't want you to think I was perverted or anything. I've never...I've never even thought of doing that before."

She closed her eyes at the erotic memory and looked at him again when he growled. She took a step away from him when he stood up, and felt a little fear when he pulled her roughly to him.

"I can smell your arousal. My tiger is racing along my skin because he wants to bite you to change you. He's very aggressive right now." She nodded and leaned back to his chest. "We're going to be more late if you don't get dressed."

"How do you change me?" His hand had been moving down her arm when it suddenly stopped. "Is there something special we have to do to get started?"

"You want to be a tiger like me?" His voice was husky, dark almost, and she nodded at him. "I would have to bite you and you'd have to want to change. I could change you without it, but I'm in enough hot water with Ryland right now."

"When?" He looked at her in the refection as she'd been doing to him. He turned her around and looked into her eyes when she asked him again.

"You're going to hurt for a while and it takes a great deal out of you." She bared her neck to him and he growled again. "You're sure? If I bite you now and it starts, there is no going back."

"I've never been surer of anything in my life as this." She licked his throat, the need to do so nearly taking her to her knees. "It's my birthday tomorrow. Can you do it tonight and I'll have reason to celebrate?"

He kissed her, and she felt all his love for her pour from him. When he let her go and leaned his head to hers, she pulled his face to hers and looked him in the eyes. She had to tell him now.

"I love you, Jules. I never thought I would but...I've got some issues and some major hang-ups, but I love you." He kissed her quickly on the nose. "That's all I get for giving you my heart?"

"No. I'll show you just how much I love you later. Right now my family is about to bust through that door, and you're naked." He swatted her ass and pushed her to the bathroom. "I would prefer that no one sees what I have, if you don't mind."

She slammed the bathroom door just as the one in the front of the little house opened. She heard Ryland roar out a command, but didn't care what it was about. She was in love and loved. He could fuck off for all she cared. When she stepped out, Sandra was standing there and no one else. She was pulling on her shoes when Sandra sat down.

"There's been another killing." She looked up in mid-tie. "Brock and Em have gone to the scene, but they would like to know if you could join them. They want your input as well."

She stood up, as did Sandra. "Where is Jules? Is he already there? I don't think anyone else should…Brock is the one with the second tiger."

"Yes. He and Em work for the Holders of the Realm. They are the ones that hunt down this sort of killer. And Jules will meet you there. Ryland needs him at your house. There has been a break-in." Before she could ask about her grandma, Sandra told her. "Your grandma is with Viktor and Peter. I guess she works for them."

Lenny had figured that out a couple of days ago. She didn't know why or what she did for them, other than be her pretend grandma, but figured it had something to do with her raising her. She'd known for some time that she wasn't any relation to her when she'd figured out her mother and father weren't human. And that they were a great deal older than they looked.

"I don't have a car." Sandra nodded and looked over her shoulder. Peter was standing there, and he didn't look happy.

"He's to take you. Bronwyn told him…she had a few words with him, and he's not happy to be pissing off Jules by touching you." Lenny was confused. "Jules is your mate and mates can get very...pissy I've heard it called...when another male touches what is theirs."

"She's making him touch me as some sort of punishment so Jules will what? Beat the shit out of him?" Sandra smiled. "That is the most asinine thing I've heard of. Would he really try to hurt him?"

"He will be allowed to." Peter put out his hand. "It is part of what I owe her. Would you like to go now? They are waiting for you."

She took his hand and nearly fell over when dizziness swamped her. She stepped away from him when they arrived at the scene, and had to grab him a second time before she felt like she could stand. She looked around and swallowed.

"It's the same thing. Just like before." She looked at Brock when he stepped toward her. "I need gloves, a note pad, and pen. And if you have a cola, I'd like that, too. It stops me from being sick on the first body." He stood staring at her. "Well, what the fuck are you waiting for? We need to process these right now."

~~~

"Four dead and all of them murdered within minutes of each other." Brock handed the file to Viktor. "The first body was found in the living room. Lenny said she was more than likely making sure the house was locked up, and whoever killed them was already in the house. The woman was eviscerated and then made up with her blood. Her lips, hair, and cheeks were saturated with it, and her intestine was used as a sort of cover for her. How the hell are they getting into the houses without being invited?"

He hadn't been thrilled to have Lenny come and help them, but she'd known more in the first five minutes than he or Em had known the entire two hours they'd been there. He handed a sheath of photos to Viktor as well as he continued with what he knew.

"The first bedroom at the top of the stairs had two kids in it. The older boy had had his neck broken and the younger had been…his head had been removed. Lenny said that was different from the first time she'd been called in. Also the blood on the lips of the wife…that and the cheeks hadn't been done to other women." He sat down and tried to breathe through what had happened to the man. "The male had been in the bathroom when he was hit the first time. He had raised his hand up, more than likely in defense, and it was removed. And she said to make sure that you knew it was removed, not cut off or even broken. It was taken off by pulling it from him. He bled a great deal as he tried to get away. There was blood on the walls where she said…. Why isn't she doing this?"

"I wondered the same thing." With a snap of his fingers, Lenny was suddenly standing in front of them. She was just putting a hotdog to her mouth when she tossed it at Viktor, and had her gun out and on him before either of them knew what was happening.

Neither man moved. Brock was pretty sure that Viktor could smell the silver in the gun. Lenny didn't drop her weapon, nor did she look like she planned on it. He moved to stand just in front of her and toward Viktor. She stopped him with a single word.

"Don't." He nodded. "You didn't tell me you worked for him. That would have been nice to know. Not to mention being transported here without a bit of notice."

"You were point on the investigation and could answer the questions better than I was. He brought you here. I'm sorry. Do you think you could put the gun down now?" She didn't move. "Lenny, he was the one that told us to bring you in. He said you'd know better than anyone what was going on."

"Of course he did. Did he also happen to mention that he was there when I was hurt? Did he tell you that he and that fucking prick Peter stood over me while I bled out?" Brock glanced at Viktor, who still hadn't moved.

"No, he didn't mention that part to us." Brock looked back at her. "Had I known, I would have let you know sooner who was footing the bills. He's not going to be happy once you put that gun down."

Brock had a feeling she didn't care. He moved out of her line of sight, but he made no move to disarm her. He was quick, but he couldn't outrun a bullet. And he was pretty sure if Viktor made a wrong move she'd shoot him just to get at the vampire.

"I know your mother, Lenore. She's the one that wants you dead." Neither of them moved and Brock thought it might be a good idea to calm his mate, as she had felt his fear and shock. As soon as Lenny had pulled the gun, Em had been all over him to tell him what the fuck was going on.

Lenny is currently pointing a gun at Viktor. She is one pissed off woman. Em snorted at him. *You will be happy to know that she's not pissed at me but at him. Apparently, he and Peter were there when she was hurt.*

Then if I was you, I'd stay the hell out of it. She's not going to be any happier with you than him if you interfere. His mate was always full of sound advice. *I'm coming to you. I have a little more information on the bodies than we had before. Tell Lenny she was right when she told us that the male had been alive when his jewels were cut off.*

He'd asked her several times not to tell him things like that. She'd done it on purpose, and he was going to have to think of ways to get back at her. Maybe he could tie her to the bed again. She'd enjoyed that a great deal and…well hell, so had he. When he started to tell Lenny what Em had found out, he realized that neither of them had moved since she'd gotten there. She had to be really tired of holding that position.

"Em said you were right on the genitals. She said that they were removed before he was dead." He sat in the chair he'd been in before she'd been brought there. "Are you going to have this going on all night? I have things to do, and sitting here watching the two of you stare at one another isn't really what I had in mind."

"Why is she trying to kill me?" Brock wanted to know as well so waited. "You said you knew her; how?"

"I helped her once a very long time ago and she had a bit of my blood. She had learned that I had certain…powers that she thought I should use for her. She said that she wanted your father released. I had taken him in and he was to serve a long sentence. But you were dying in your bedding. I don't believe you'd had nutriment for several days." The gun lowered, but Brock didn't doubt that she could bring it up and fire it on a second's notice. "She gave you to me. As part of the deal, I was to have your father released. And in return I took something from her."

Brock couldn't imagine giving up a child for any reason, but to simply give her away was something he found to be sickening. He looked at Lenny when she holstered the weapon. She sat down on the edge of the seat and bounced her foot. He'd noticed today when they were working together that she did it when she was thinking.

"I did some digging and found that neither of them was human. What were they? And don't give me any bullshit answer that they were special. I don't think of them as special unless you count the amount of times the Holders had them and then let them go." Brock looked at Viktor, who appeared to be surprised by her knowing about the were's council, too. "Why didn't you just rid us of them then?"

"You know as well as I do that rules must be followed to the letter or some things…I cannot remember the right wording, but 'bite you in the ass,' I believe it goes." He smiled and Brock had a feeling he didn't care for the rules either. "It is why we could not interfere with you at the house. Your mother would have claimed that I saved you so that she would lose her powers. As it was, when I gave you a few drops we were messing with things that were better left untouched."

"You skirted around that pretty good, giving me other information you think I want. When what I want to know is what the hell was I spawned from?" Viktor sat back, and Lenny stood up to pace.

"What did you find out? I cannot give you more than you have. I will be truthful to you on every question that is not a fishing one. Asking me what they were will not give what you seek. And you were not spawned of anyone, but born of two beings that did the world a favor by breeding." She stopped pacing long enough to stare. "You will have great power once you reach your maturity."

"Power? I don't want any power. I have enough shit going on in my life without having something I can't control or, for that matter, want. When is this supposed to happen? When some blood-drinking prick like you sinks his teeth into me?" Brock was surprised by the venom in her voice, but could understand why she was upset. They'd let her lay there and hurt without doing anything.

"Tonight at midnight." Brock stood when she swayed a little, and when the door crashed against the wall behind him, he wasn't surprised to see Jules coming through it as his tiger. Brock's own beast was trying to get free and he was barely holding him when Viktor stood and raised his hand. Everything froze, including his brother in mid-leap.

"Stop this at once." Viktor's voice echoed in the room. "You will sit and listen to me. I have a great deal to tell you all, and this bantering back and forth as if we are parlaying with swords is getting us nowhere."

Jules settled to the floor near Lenny, but he didn't shift once Viktor sat down again. Brock wasn't sure if it was because he'd be naked or that he still wanted to tear the vampire's throat out. The beast inside of him was doing a number on his insides, and he wasn't any happier than Viktor looked right now. The man nearly glowed with ill-suppressed anger.

"Now. I will tell you what you need to know for this night. The rest will come later when there is more time. I swear to you, Lenore, that it was not my intention to have her try and murder you when I struck the deal with her." Lenny nodded at Viktor. "Her name was Divinity when I last knew her, but recently I found out her name is Naomi. She is coming for you because if you do not reach your twenty-fifth birthday, she will not lose all her powers. She has it in her head that killing you will make a difference."

"Will it?" Brock waited for an answer as Lenny and Viktor stared at one another. When he finally turned to him, he knew the answer immediately.

"It will make no difference concerning her powers, no, but it will make a difference to what the Holders of the Realm do to her if she succeeds in killing Lenore. But I'm hoping that she doesn't get that far. I believe that with this family behind her and what she has gained by mating with Jules that there will be no chance of Naomi beating her."

"But you won't help me again." Viktor shook his head at Lenny. "So once again you're leaving me to the wolves to die."

"I leave you with everything you need, my dear child. It is up to you to figure out how best to use what you have."

Chapter 12

Sam watched the house of the tiger. There had been no movement since he'd arrived and he could smell that there were people inside. When a woman had arrived a little over an hour ago, he had nearly come out from his hiding place to grab her, but she'd turned and looked right where he was. He knew she couldn't see him, but he had a feeling she knew he was out there somewhere. Stepping back into the woods, he watched her remove a car seat from the back of the vehicle and take it into the house. A few minutes later, she and the car seat left. He could only assume that a child was in it both times, but wasn't sure.

He turned in the drive as another large SUV pulled up in front of the house. He'd been concentrating on the house and wondering how best to get inside, and didn't hear the vehicle until it was going past him. He tried to see how many people were inside as the thing simply sat in the drive with the engine running. He was ready to move closer when he felt something touch the back of his head.

"Move and I will gladly put a bullet through your head." His gun in his hand was suddenly gone. "We're going to move slowly out of the woods here and you're going to walk ahead of me. And just so you know, there are five tigers surrounding your fucking ass right now, and any of them would gladly tear you apart."

"I'm not alone." He was but thought if he could get at least two of the big cats he could now see to leave, he could maybe take on the one behind him and the others. The laughter made him think the guy knew he was lying.

"My wife says you work alone and prefer it that way. She also said to tell you that you smell of vampire and that she personally wants to give you a hose down. My wife is a little on the pissed side right now. She doesn't like to be spied on." The gun hit him hard enough to make him move forward. "Who sent you? As if we don't already know."

Sam tried to think. The gun was full of silver and the cats were on full alert and pissed. He thought he'd stand at least a small chance to get free, which to him was better than what they had in store for him, when the big bear stood in front of him. And right next to him was the biggest fucking tiger Sam had ever seen. The thing was at least a head taller than the others, and his muscle mass alone had to be more than his as a human.

When the gun hit him again, he realized he'd stopped moving. Before he could take another step, the big tiger roared at him.

"This is my brother. Brock is mad because you're still alive. He had hoped that one of us would have killed you. But as the male, I thought maybe I'd hold off on that for a few minutes." The bone-chilling laughter again. "I thought maybe you'd like to meet Lenny."

The girl. He didn't move when she stepped from behind the tiger. They stared at one another for several seconds before she spoke, and when she did, he felt fear, more than he'd ever experienced before, run over his skin like a flame.

"Let them kill him." He felt the gun press harder into his skull, and Sam knew that the male would let them kill him and it would be a slow and very painful death. Without a second thought as a matter of fact.

"I'll tell you whatever you want to know. I don't know where she's staying right now, but I know it's close." The girl started to turn her back, and he was knocked to his knees. "She is planning another family to be murdered tonight in hopes that you'll go to the scene again. Once you're there, she will have the rogues snatch you up and bring you to her. She has this huge ceremony planned out where she removes your head after she tears you apart."

"Where?" He told her he didn't know. "Then you're not a great deal of use to me, are you?"

"I know I can find the rogues. I have their scent. I can take you to the lair." He looked at the tiger at her right, smaller than the beast but no less willing to tear him apart. "They are both at the cemetery. She wouldn't let them stay in her home because she can't stand them. She's not their maker."

"And this information is helpful to me how?" Sam glanced at the man behind him, then back at her when she continued. "You have five seconds before I release them. You say something fucking helpful and I won't let him kill you. Otherwise, you're going to be lunch for them, and I will gladly watch you die."

"She won't know when you kill them. Once they're dead, nobody has to die. The family will be safe. You'll be safe from them, as will the cops that would be working the scene with you." The girl looked to her right, and he saw a man standing there. Sam swallowed twice. He knew this man, Viktor Ravengric. He was with the Holders of the Realm, and was someone really high on the food chain, too, if he remembered correctly.

"What he says is true. She will not feel their passing." Viktor looked at him. "You should have said no to this contract, Samuel Lamb."

No shit, he thought. The girl watched him closely, and he wondered what was going through her mind. When she nodded, he was suddenly being jerked to a standing position and set back on his feet when he stumbled. A pair of silver handcuffs was put at his wrists and a pair of shackles at his legs. He couldn't run now if his life depended on it, which he was pretty sure it was going to come to. He watched her walk toward him with a tiger on either side of her. The bear was ambling toward him as well. The man with the gun still had it pointed at his head, but it was no longer feeling as if he were trying to insert it into his skull.

"Where are they resting?" He shook his head. He wasn't stupid enough to just give up his only bargaining tool. If he told her, she'd simply have the guy with the gun shoot him.

"I want assurances that you won't kill me or have this ambush kill me." She looked over his shoulder, and he knew she was looking at the male. "He can tell me all he wants, but it's you I'm going to trust."

The gun banged him in the head. "She doesn't know what an ambush is, as we go by streak. And I won't lie to you either, you fucking moron. I want this finished now so I can move on with my fucking life. An ambush is just another name for a streak. I prefer streak over ambush myself, as it is kinder sounding and much less harsh sounding when you say it. Ambush implies that I'm going to attack you, which, under normal circumstances, I won't. But this idiot...." He hit him again. "I would gladly ambush him anytime."

"Thanks, Ryland." She looked at Sam and her entire face changed from a sweet smile to hatred in less time than it did for his heart to beat. "I won't kill you, and I won't allow the streak to kill you either, unless you're lying to me or you try something stupid like getting away. Or you simply piss me off again. I'm sick to fucking death of being chased, lied to, and generally forced into a bad mood. Deal?"

He nodded. Christ, she was hard. He wondered if any of the cats were her mate and hoped to Christ not. They were going to be really fucking pissed off when they found out that the lair that he was taking them to was full of vampires, not just the two they were after.

He told her the name of the cemetery as well as the mausoleum they were inside of. He watched as three of the tigers suddenly disappeared, along with the girl. When the gun disappeared as well, he knew the male had gone, too. Sam started to stand when Viktor was jerking him to his feet.

"They run into trouble, young pup, and I will personally feed you to the pits of hell on my own." Sam felt his body being lifted up and he was tossed against a tree. Bones broke as he landed hard against it and then fell to the ground. When he was lifted again, he tried to speak but nothing was working. But Viktor had no such problems.

"You made a deal with the wrong person, cub. Lenore has no authority at all when it comes to what becomes of you. You belong to me and the Realm now." He was slammed against another tree and held there this time. "When I take you in me, I must be assured that no harm will come to the others on the governing group. I am rendering you unable to harm anyone you might encounter."

Sam had never been one to pray, but he did now; first, for the girl and her group that nothing woke while they were there; and, secondly, for his own death. He was pretty sure that dying by the tigers would have been faster than what this man and the others he worked with were going to do to him. More than likely it would be much worse.

~~~

"Wait." Lenny didn't know why but she had a feeling they were walking into a trap. She looked at the cats, not really sure who they were but for Brock, who was a fucking monster, and Jules. He rubbed his head against her leg, and she felt a sort of calmness roll over her.

What is it? You think he lied about them being here? It's daylight...they won't be able to hurt us, right? She shook her head at Neal and looked back at the large brick building.

"They won't be able to hurt us unless we wake them. And we'd have to kill them both at the same time or the one that was last could kill us." She looked back at the cats. "One of you is Bronwyn, right?"

The cat moved toward her, as did a second one. Ryland pointed out which one was his mate and said the other was Rayne. He said they could help.

"I want you to ask them if there are more than two vampires inside. I don't trust the bastard, and for all we know this place could be crawling with the creepy things." She shivered and glared at Ryland when he laughed. "I don't know about you, big boy, but the thought of going into a den of vampires is not on my list of top ten things to do today."

"Mine either, but Rayne said you were smart and she admired you." She didn't know why he thought that was funny and told him. "Well, Bronwyn said you are smarter than she is. And she's impressed. She doesn't say that of too many people."

Nodding, Lenny turned back to the den. She was embarrassed by the praise and didn't want any of them to see it. When Rayne and Bronwyn stepped to the building and stood against it, she realized how fucking big they were.

You'll be that beautiful, more so I think. She felt Jules rub her leg again. *I want nothing more than to take you back to our bed and show you just how much you mean to me. I want to take you against the shower wall again. I want to lick you until you come screaming my name. Then when you can shift, I'm going to let my tiger run you down and bury his cock deep inside of you and fill you with our seed.*

Jules growled low, and she felt it as if he'd actually touched her with it. When his head was under her hand, she buried her fingers into his thick fur and felt his purr beneath them. She was nearly to the point where she wanted to beg him to shift and take her when the two female cats pulled away from the wall. Ryland cleared his throat.

"There are twenty-three vampires in the den. All of them young, and one who hasn't killed a human, because he's only been a vamp since last night. He's not had his first rising yet." She looked at the den, then back at the two cats. "They have more information if you want it."

"No. No, I think that's enough." Now what? They couldn't enter now without one or more of them getting hurt. She looked at the place and then at the cats. She smiled.

"What do you think about lifting the roof off this sucker?" Ryland walked around it and looked at the cats. Peter was suddenly there, too. He looked like he'd just won the lottery.

"I may be of assistance with this one." He dropped several small duffels. "There are clothes there enough for each of you. I believe that as humans you would have more luck with this than as cats."

They all walked behind the big brick building and shifted. As they each came around it, she realized just how close they were. When they were all standing there, Peter said he could help her again. She watched as he lifted each man to the top. She had no idea how this was going to work, or even if it would, but they had to do something. Ally came and stood next to her and smiled.

"I would have blown the building. Then we'd have all been blown to bits because of it. I asked Rayne what she would have done, and she said that setting it on fire was her way of killing them. Messy, though, I think. Em said that she would have gone in with guns blazing, but again, not very smart. As you said, when one woke, they all would have." Lenny looked at her, wanting to know what Bronwyn would have done. "She said she would have waited for you to come up with a brilliant plan that none of them would have gotten bitten or killed from. She's a major suck up, by the way."

Lenny didn't understand what she'd have to suck up about. She was nothing compared to any of these women. And she was a little afraid they weren't going to be as accepting come midnight. She watched as the men were ready to do their thing. It seemed that Peter had gone and gotten them all sledgehammers and they were going to break it in. The door to the front had been secured by silver dust that Viktor had sent along with Peter as well.

"Viktor told me he was taking Sam, the wolf, to the Holders. He said that the man would be begging before they were finished with him. He has a great many crimes to pay for." Ally nodded at her as she continued. "He wants me to trust him."

"I know. He told us that he'd like to help you, but he wasn't sure you'd ever trust him again. Did he explain to you why he didn't help you in the house?" Lenny nodded. "It must have been very hard on him to see you laying there all cut up. I don't know what I'd have done had that been my child."

"I'm not his kid." Ally nodded. "He just saved me from starving to death as a kid by sending me away from my mother. She would have probably killed me eventually, I suppose, but he sent me away."

"He gave you his blood." She looked at Bronwyn when she spoke. "When he took you from your mother, you were as close to death as possible without actually being dead. She'd not fed you for several days, Nicee told me. And you were dirty and wet, sores on your body from neglect and filthy conditions. You only survived because he gave you a chance."

"My father had been in prison, she told me, along with my mother. But the Realm had them. And they let her go after he died." The hammering started then, and she looked up. "I never found out what they'd done to end up there. They were both set to be executed the next day before he died was all I was able to find out."

"Your mother would lure men to their home and have sex with them while your father and their watcher, a man named Milo, watched. Then when the male or female lay basking in the afterglow, Milo would tie them to the bed with a promise of more to come. Once they were secured, your father would come out and he'd...he was a sadist. He and your mother both were. Milo liked to watch them, she said, but they were the ones that did all the killing. They had killed nearly two dozen humans before the Realm caught up with them." Em handed her a folded sheet of paper. "Your father was sixty-three years old when he died. Your mother is nine hundred and forty-five. She was converted when she was about your age. Her maker met the sun just after she was changed. The Realm now thinks she had a part in it." Lenny opened the file and saw her first picture of her parents.

She didn't look a thing like her mother, who was shorter than her and very thin. Her hair was dark, too, almost blue in the photo. But even in the photograph, Lenny could see her evilness and wondered why she'd been released to the general public.

However, she was her father's daughter. Red flaming hair, green eyes, and tall, he looked like a Viking. She wondered how two people so completely opposite in looks could have come together to create her.

She started to hand it back to Em when she told her to keep it. She wadded it up and tossed it to the ground.

"I don't want any reminders of what I came from. I want to find the fucking bitch and ram a stake through her heart, and laugh while she incinerates. If Daddy was around, I'd empty a clip of silver in his head, then reload and fucking take his heart out." Em smiled. "I'm not joking."

"Oh, I know that. It's good to see that you're ready to destroy them. I know that killing your parents is somewhat frowned upon." They both looked at Rayne when she laughed. "But as you know, neither of them would be getting the good parent award, and I think killing the cunt will be healthy for you."

The screaming started before she could say anything. The door to the front was barred, but that didn't stop the vampires on the other side from trying their best to open it. Several of them even tried flying out of the openings that were being made, only to burst into flames before they were even cleared of the destruction. Then when the roof came down completely, there was a sudden and abrupt silence.

"They are no more." Lenny sat down, her knees suddenly very weak. When Peter grabbed her before she could fall over, she looked up at him as he continued. "My lady, you did the Realm a great service today. Killing off these rogues has saved countless lives. We are indebted to you and yours."

She nodded, not sure what to say about murdering that many people, but saw Jules coming toward her. As he dropped his hammer and continued toward her, she stood up. He scooped her up into his arms before she could tell him she loved him.

Lenny held him to her as the others talked. She was sure she should pay attention to what they were saying, but right now she needed to be held. When he lifted her chin up and kissed her mouth, she smiled at him.

"You all right?" She nodded at him. "You saved a great many people with this idea. I'm very proud of you."

"I love you." He purred at her, and she smiled. "You do know how much that turns me on, right?"

"Yes. It's what I live for." He wrapped his arms around her tighter. "I've spoken to Ryland, and he's given me permission to change you. Not that I really needed it, but I wanted to do this right for us. You still want this, right?"

"More than ever. How long will it take? I mean, can we start right now?" He shook his head. "I'd really like to meet Mommy with a little extra on my side if it's all the same to you."

"You'd be too weak at midnight even if she waited that long. No, when we do this, it's going to be done properly and without any other reason other than we both want it."

She nodded, but really was worried about going up against her mother. Lenny wasn't really afraid of her, but now that she had found Jules and happiness, she didn't really want to die. Not that she had before, but now she had more of a reason to live. She walked with him to the back of the destroyed graveyard for so many vampires and waited for their turn to be taken back to the house. She decided it was time she had a talk with Viktor.

Chapter 13

"You'll feel the power come to you at midnight tonight, just as the hands touch the twelve. Your mother will feel the same, but she will lose what you gain." Viktor waited to make sure the young couple understood what he was telling them. "You'll feel a slight dizziness, I would imagine, but nothing that you won't be able to conquer in a very short time."

"What is it I'll get?" Viktor looked at Jules and wondered if the man needed a moment more, but he nodded and looked at his mate. Viktor was sure the man didn't understand him and, for that matter, neither did the girl. He decided to not tell them what was really going to happen, but let them believe it was only the girl getting this gift.

"I am not completely sure." She cocked a brow at him and he smiled. "What I mean is that I'm not sure what you'll get from either of them. Nor how much you'll receive from them. You may receive more of what your father gave you or your mother, depending, I suppose, on what your body can handle. Power unlike you've ever seen is what I think, but as I said, I'm not sure."

"So, let me get this straight. At midnight tonight I'm going to come into this awesome power that you don't know what it is and you don't know how much it will be. You have no idea if I'll get all of it or just a small portion from either of my sires. Not to mention you're not sure really how hard it's going to be on me when it does come to me. I mean, I could just be dizzy or I might just keel over. Fuck, that's not good, is it?" He didn't get a chance to answer her as she continued on her harangue. "Did I forget anything? Oh wait, my mother is trying to kill me before all this happens so she won't be helpless as she lives out the rest of her life as a murdering bitch fixated on only herself and how all this concerns her."

He wanted to laugh at her or at the very least smile, but he feared that she would harm him. A great deal as a matter of fact. He leaned back in the chair and decided perhaps a different approach might be in order. She certainly wasn't appreciating his tact.

"You're a strong woman, so most of what they give you will cause you no harm at all. Your father was a shifter, but not necessarily all that talented at it. He could take on the shape of the animal, but he could not become one. He was too set on his way of making things work out for himself instead of the benefit of what he could do with his talent. He could also, after he was converted by your mother, transport. Not the same as willing himself over a great distance by using his mind, but he could move his body, and that of someone he was touching, over great distances without worrying about what might be in his path when he arrived...you know, a chair or something. Peter can do something similar, but he must be worried that something, a tree or a table leg for instance, will be in his way when he gets there. Nasty business, that, if a sliver of wood should be where he was landing." He watched her face and could see that this was getting through to her. "Your mother, however, has a great deal more to offer you. She is old and as she has aged, her powers came to her with that. She cannot, of course, stand much in the way of sunlight, but more so than a younger vampire. She can go great lengths of time without feeding, though I believe she does kill her...meals rather than pay for their services."

"I might be a vampire." Viktor didn't answer her, for he knew she was going to at least have fangs, as both her sires had. "If that happens, what happens to Jules and I when I have to feed?"

"You will simply feed from him, but I would caution you about thinking that would happen. Vampires do have children, as you are well aware, but the likelihood of you needing to feed to survive...I believe that will not happen."

"But you don't know." He told her no, he did not. "These powers that she has, what else is there? I mean, can she shift, fly, or any of those other things that you read about that vampires can do?"

"Fly, in a matter of speaking, yes. She can levitate herself to great heights. She can shift, but I do not think that she cares for it and does it only to heal herself." He looked at Jules. "You shift to heal, correct?"

"Yes. Whether we're in human or cat form, if we shift, we're healed. Not mortal wounds, but ones that are bad. Broken legs, arms, deep cuts, and even bad burns can be fixed by shifting." He looked at Lenny before looking at him again. "This thing with her mother, you know the outcome, don't you? I get the feeling you know the outcome of a great deal."

Viktor couldn't lie to him; he had made a promise. "I do know a great deal, but for this I only know what the outcome could be either way. Should Lenny win, the two of you will have several children over your lifetimes together and live a long and very happy life. Should her mother win and kill her, then you, too, will be killed and the world as we know it will be changed forever."

"How?" He looked at Lenny, and she frowned. "Fishing question. Okay, I get it. You say the world will change. Will it be a better place? I don't know how it could, but I can ask."

"It will not." Viktor waited, knowing that she would have to ask. It was in her body and he could see it on her face. She would need to know.

"If Jules doesn't go with me to challenge her, will—?"

"I will not leave you to do this on your own no matter the outcome. I love you and I won't abandon you when you need me the most." Jules pulled her into his arms. "Don't even think about it, Lenny. If I have to, I'll lock you into a room where she can't get to you until this is over."

"He will die regardless of whether you go alone or not. And your chances of survival will be much improved if he does go with you." He looked at Jules again. "While I can commend your thinking that locking her away will solve this, it will not. She will simply be where Divinity can get to her easier and kill her as well. You and your mate stand the best chance by going full steam ahead."

When the grandfather clock in the other room started its chime, both of them tensed. Viktor could feel the pull of the moon as well as any paranormal did. He knew that it was close to four in the afternoon. They had about three hours before her mother rose for the night.

When he stood up, the couple did as well. "I would ask that you go home and rest. It will be a long and hard night, and you need to be relaxed and without stress." He winked at Jules. "Surely, young man, you can use a nice nap as well." When he nodded, Viktor snapped his fingers and they both disappeared.

"They will survive, you think?" Peter walked in the room as he spoke. "The Realm has already given her a bit of her powers for the work she did for them today. It will give them an edge that they will need, I think."

Viktor nodded and looked at Peter. "My brother comes in two weeks. He would like to meet the Golden family. When this is through, we will need to make sure that the younger boy meets his mate before then. They need to be all together when the madness starts."

"Yes. Will you play them as you did the young Bronwyn? It was not very sporting of you to allow me to tell her that young Lenore was Jules's mate." Viktor flushed, knowing that what he did bordered on cheating. "You will do the same for young Keith?"

"I will do what is necessary to ensure this family is safe beyond all others. You know what they did for us." Peter nodded and sat down. "You also know that if anyone should find out what we've done that hell will be paid."

"I'm willing to pay it." Peter said so without any hesitation, just as Viktor thought he would. They both owed the Goldens more than they'd ever be able to repay. They settled into their seats to wait. They would be there when the mother and daughter met, and would remain there until word came to them of the outcome.

"I think I shall need a vacation after this. I was thinking perhaps we would venture home for a visit. Maybe a decade or two. What do you think, my friend?" Peter nodded but his mind was elsewhere. Not that he blamed him; a great deal rested on this night.

~~~

Their bodies came together as if they'd both been in the same frame of mind. He tore at her clothes as she did his. As soon as they were both naked, he picked her up and pressed her against the wall. She wrapped her legs around him as he filled her with his cock.

"Don't hold back. Come for me. I need to feel you come around me." He pounded into her, the wall behind her shaking as pictures fell to the floor. "Come. Christ, come now."

She shook her head and jerked his head back. "No. I need to taste you. I want to feel you come in my mouth; I want you to fuck me like that until you come."

He was suddenly with his back to the wall and her at his feet. He wanted to tell her that she could later, but they both knew there might not be a later. He watched her lick his cock from balls to tip. She looked up at him as she took him into her hot mouth.

"Fuck, that's it." Her tongue curled around him, circling around the crown of his cock so many times he was sure she had more than one tongue. As she cupped his balls and rolled them gently in her hands, he rocked into her heat. When she pulled him closer to her and swallowed him, he nearly cried out from the tightness of her throat around his already sensitive cock. Cupping the back of her head and holding her there, he pumped as gently as he could into her. She wasn't having it.

The moment she nipped at him he felt his climax race up his spine until he could almost taste it in the back of his throat. When she gave his balls a small twist, he cried out even as his cum spewed from him. He couldn't have stopped fucking her like this now if there was a gun to his head. When she licked him along his cock to his balls, he nearly snarled at her when she took one, then the other into her mouth.

"Enough love. I need to fuck you." She lifted her head from his cock and stared at him as if she were drugged. He knew just how she felt. As he stood her up, he kissed her deeply as he moved her backward toward the bed. When she touched the edge, he lifted her into his arms and dropped her onto it. He was on top of her before she was finished bouncing.

"I love the taste of you." He licked her throat as she continued. "The way you feel fucking me like that. I want to do that again and again."

"And I'll allow it. Now, however, it's my turn." Moving down her body, he kissed her everywhere he could. She tasted of his soap and sweat, of sex and the earth. He wanted more than anything to savor her, but he also needed her. When he reached her naval, a place he knew her to be ticklish, he laved his tongue inside of her, then lifted his head.

"I love you." She nodded. "No, I really do love you. I never wanted…I thought I never wanted a mate, much less one like you…independent, opinionated, and strong. I wanted a mate that I could order around and make her do what I thought best."

"You nearly had to go and find you one of those, the way you were acting." He nodded. "But I guess I'll keep you now. You can do all those amazing things with your hands. I think your pottery pieces are lovely."

"My pottery pieces, huh?" She nodded and he moved to the edge of the bed, pretending to leave her. But they both knew he wasn't going anywhere.

"You mold them so well with your strong hands." She sat up behind him, and he could feel her breasts rub along his back. Her hands ran down his chest, and he ached for her to touch him. "Tomorrow night you're going to change me and I'm going to be your tigress. When you chase me through the woods, I'm going to let you find me so you can do all the things to me that your cat wants to."

He turned and pulled her into his arms and across his lap. He kissed her gently, then held her to him. He wanted to say so much to her, but he was afraid of breaking down. She needed his support right now, not him blubbering like a fool.

"I want to marry you as soon as it's possible. Then when you go into heat I want to have children with you. Lots and lots of children." She nodded. "Lenny, we're going to do this. We're going to show your mother what it's like to fuck with a Golden."

He rolled her back to the bed and kissed her. He needed to make love to her in the worst way. Moving down her body again, he touched her, ran his hands over her smooth body. When she sighed, he kissed her again and slowly, reverently entered her.

"Mine. You're all mine." She moaned and lifted her hips up to his thrust. "Say it, Lenny, say you're all mine."

"I love you. I belong to you. All of me." She gripped his shoulders as she threw back her head and screamed. His entire body seemed to be poised for her next climax. His cat snarled at him to mark her, to come in her and make her his. Before he could think what he was doing, he sank his teeth into her throat and bit her hard as his cock released deep and hard, and he knew immediately his mistake.

Her scream ripped through him, but he couldn't stop. When he started to lift his head, she held him to her and begged him to finish. She knew what he was doing and there was no way he could let her go now. When he felt the change in her start, he knew that something wasn't right. She was going to be his cat much sooner than he'd ever thought. Lifting his head, he looked down at her and she smiled. He felt his heart skip several beats when she closed her eyes.

"Baby, I'm so sorry. I didn't...I knew when I bit you that I shouldn't have. It's too soon. I'm so sorry, honey." She patted him gently on the cheek, and he saw a tear race down her own. He kissed it away and watched as another formed.

"I love you and it will be fine. I need to be as strong as I can to win, and you're going to help me." She smiled again. "I belong to you, all of me."

He held her for over an hour. He wasn't sure what to do, but he had to hold onto her. If anything happened to her because of this, he would never forgive himself. Never.

He heard his cell phone ringing and got up to look for it. He answered it and waited for the person on the other end to speak.

"You're not her." He looked at the caller ID and didn't recognize the number. "No matter. You must be close to her or you wouldn't have heard the phone ring."

"Who is this?" The laughter at the other end made his cat snarl. He waited for an answer while he jerked on his pants. Something was way off about this.

The simple command made him dizzy. As she repeated the word *"Come"* to him, he felt his body seem to weaken, then blackness took him. As he faded out, he reached for Ryland.

I'm in trouble. Come to the apartment. His brother said he'd be there, to hang on. *I can't. I think…I think her mother is bringing me to her.*

The room he was suddenly in was aglow with candle light. Every flat surface and even some that didn't look all that flat had a candle glowing from it. When he tried to stand, a woman appeared in front of him. He had figured she was the one, but now that he could see her, he knew.

"You won't win. She's going to defeat you and you're going to be nothing but a fucking human." She grinned at him. "You'll see when she comes for me. You'll see that you're going to lose."

"Oh, she'll come for you all right. I'm hoping for that. But will she be here in time is the question you should be asking yourself. If she finds the message in time, you'll live. If not…." She shrugged at him. "You really should have more clothing on, dear. Where I plan to hold you is going to be very cold on your skin."

She touched him and he jerked away. When he tried to move from her, she lifted her hand and his raised as well. Before he could figure out her intent, she had him chained to the wall with silver chains. Then he watched in horror as chains crawled across the floor like snakes and lifted up to look at him. He could have sworn that they hissed at him, but they moved to his ankles and wrapped tightly around them.

She paced the room several times before she came back to him. He wasn't sure what to expect, but he figured she was going to make him suffer a great deal before anyone could come here. He reached for his brother, not trusting the woman in front of him, to try and find Lenny with his mind. He wasn't really surprised to find the link blocked by something.

"Can you reach her?" He didn't answer, and she put her hand on him again. He cried out in pain as she raked claws down his chest. "I asked you a question, and I do expect you to answer me. I'm not accustomed to people treating me poorly."

"But you're okay with you treating others poorly." That earned him another claw mark down his chest, and he hissed through the pain this time. "I don't know who you're talking about."

"Don't be an imbecile. My daughter. Can you reach her?" She paced again after licking her fingers of his blood. "I wish I still had something of hers."

She hadn't a clue who her daughter was. That thought rolled in his head several times as he watched her mutter to herself and pace. When finally she stopped and looked at him, he couldn't help it; he laughed.

"You have no idea who she is, do you? For all you know, any female that walks through the door could be her." She glared at him, and he laughed harder. "You really are the perfect mother, aren't you? You'll be put up for mother of the year when this is over."

"Shut up." He continued to laugh but calmed a little when she strode toward him. "She was stolen from me when she was an infant. I don't...someone took her from me, and now I just want to be reunited with her."

"You mean Viktor." She stood perfectly still and he knew he'd hit a nerve. "He tells a different story than you having your daughter stolen away. He said you nearly killed her with neglect. Did you?"

"You have no idea what happened to me during that time." She started pacing again. "Her mate, it's not Viktor, is it? That would be just a bitch."

He wanted to tell her that he was her mate but didn't. Instead, he looked around where they were. It was a lair. He was in her lair and that was why he couldn't reach anyone. When she came toward him again, he thought she was going to ask him more about her daughter. Instead, she pulled out a long knife and stabbed him in the chest with it. As the room began to fade, he heard her laugh. Then her voice seemed to echo in his head.

You should have simply let her answer the fucking phone and you'd be safe in your nice little house. She jerked his head up. "What's her name? What's the fucking bitch's name?"

Warm liquid poured over his chest and he felt his cat snarl. He couldn't shift, not with his hands and feet chained. When his head lolled to his chest, he saw his blood pour from him even as she screamed at him to answer her. He did eventually. Knowing that he was dying and didn't much care what she thought of him, he lifted his head and told her.

"Her name is Fuck You." The pain radiated from his head to his entire body. When he reached out this time, he felt Viktor telling him to hold on, that help was on the way. It was too late for him. He knew that, and he was pretty sure that Viktor did as well. When his vision blurred to the point he couldn't see a damned thing, he let it take him, but not before giving Viktor a message to give to his mate.

I love her. Will you tell her that I love her very much, and that she will be in my heart for all of time? He told him again to hang on. *I wish we had made a child. I would love for her to have had my child.*

He calmed his cat as he, too, began to die. This was not how he'd thought his end would come. He'd thought...hell, he'd never thought. Closing his eyes, Jules thought of his mom and his family. They were going to be so pissed when they found out.

Chapter 14

She knew that pacing the floor wasn't getting her anywhere, but she needed to do something. She watched as Viktor and Peter spoke to Keith and when he looked at her, she tried to smile. It was her fault that their brother had been taken, and she had to get him back. She turned to Sandra.

"I'm going to go and get him." Sandra raised a brow at her. "I can't just sit around here and wait for him to die because it's still an hour before midnight."

"And just where will you go? Do you have some sort of tracking system that will lead you to him? Or her for that matter? If you do, I'd very much like to use it when I go to the mall. I'm forever losing my car in the lot. Will you please sit down?"

She sat but wasn't happy. She was seriously pissed off, and she wanted someone to feel it. When Brock walked by her, she wanted to trip him so he would fight with her, but he turned to her at the last second and smiled.

"He won't play fairly, and I'm pretty sure that he'd hurt you a great deal more than you can afford right now." He winked at her. "You and I will play later."

"She has him and I want him back." He nodded and sat near her. "Please just let me go and find him. I'm sure that she's close. Peter said she couldn't have pulled him to her for a long distance the way she took him."

"Here you go." She took the small piece of paper. "Em and Bronwyn are already in the yard. Ryland is too. Go out through the kitchen and slip into the yard beyond the pool house. Mom said you know where it is."

She glanced down at the address and then up at him. He stood up and moved toward the kitchen himself. She supposed they were gathering forces, but she wasn't sure why they were doing it so quietly. She looked over at Sandra when she sat next to her.

"The Realm, dear. They are not allowing anyone to go find Jules because they think to save you over him." Lenny looked at her, not believing that. "They said it would be for the best. I'd very much like to show them my best. My best fist in the nose. Who are they to say who lives or dies?"

She didn't know and looked at the kitchen door. She had to hurry now and needed to get going. When Sandra stood up and swayed slightly, Lenny started to reach for her but didn't when she nodded toward the kitchen. She was giving her a diversion. As soon as Sandra moved closer to the three men and further away from her, she swayed again, this time managing to pull off a beautiful vase filled with flowers.

Lenny was through the kitchen door when she heard Viktor yell to grab her. Laughing, Lenny ran across the yard to the pool house to find all of them there, with the exception of Keith.

"He'll be along shortly. He found the address about twenty minutes ago and gave it to me." Ryland took off his shirt. "We're going to run across the fields as tigers. It's much quicker that way. You're going to as well. Are you ready for this?"

Was she? She looked at Ryland, just realizing that he knew. She backed up, fearful that he'd be pissed because they hadn't waited.

"You take this out on him when I get him back, and so help me you'll have to sleep with both eyes open and I'll still get back at you. It was entirely my fault anyway. I wanted this and he didn't have a choice. You want to be pissed then you take it—"

He put his hand over her mouth. "While I would normally have fun at your expense, we don't really have time for this. I'm not mad. And the fact that you're ready to go without any signs of weakness means there is something more going on with you than this thing with your mother. Now, are you ready?"

She nodded and he handed her a robe. He told her to go behind the tree and take off her clothes, and when she was undressed to put on the robe and come back. He told her she would need her clothes when they got to the house. She was just pulling on the robe when Keith came toward them. He was smiling.

"Man, Mom should get an award for her performance. She had those men trying everything to get her to sit down." He looked at her. "You ready there, sis?"

"I have no idea." He nodded at her, and she wanted to beg him to help her but he only took her clothes and put them into a duffle. Then he showed her how to tie it around her.

"It'll come off easily if you're caught. Now, I want you to close your eyes and think of your cat. It might hurt a little, but just think of a tiger, your tiger, and let her come—"

Closing her eyes again, she let the tiger come to her. It was strange to see something so vicious and so large looking at her with such awe. When Lenny smiled at her, the cat, beautiful in her white coat, waved her large paw at her in a sort of greeting. When she nodded, the cat seemed to leap at her and she felt the sudden fear, then…nothing. She opened her eyes to see that the others had shifted, and she was disappointed that she would not be able to keep up.

She's white. She opened her eyes and looked at Keith. *That can't be right, can it? A white tiger?*

It is if that's what you are. Ryland laughed a little as he looked at her and answered Keith. *I've only ever seen one other white tiger, and she's standing over there. Bronwyn isn't really white but she can shift to one. So can Rayne. But you're not a shifter, and if your tiger is white, then she's white. Bring her out to play with us, Lenny. I want my brother home.* Ryland came to her, and he touched her mind again.

You're lovely. She shook her head and he laughed. *You're all white. A very rare completely white tiger. You're called a royal white, and I'm honored to have you in my streak.* When he bowed before her, she wanted to run and find a mirror.

I didn't think it worked. She took a step forward and nearly fell over. *Wow, that's weird. I guess walking on four feet is harder than I thought.*

It was hard to walk and learn how to step at first. She kept tangling her back feet up with her hands…front feet, she supposed…and kept falling over. No one laughed at her but were all very encouraging. She looked up at Ryland and told him to go on and she'd catch up.

We stick together in this. Besides, I want to see Jules's face when you shift in front of your mother. He watched her a few more minutes before he told her she had it. *You should also know that you're bigger than a normal cat. Nearly half again the size of Bronwyn and the other females. Not as big as Em's beast, but close. You're going to kick her ass if you have to shift to take her.*

They were running, and she had to concentrate hard on doing it. As soon as she leapt over the first fallen log, she laughed. It was an amazing feeling to soar over something and land so nicely. She didn't even feel winded when Ryland stopped in front of her. Alistair — she knew which tiger was which now — stepped beside her and nudged her shoulder.

You'll need to touch each of us as a cat to communicate with us. Do you know us in this form? She told him she did, surprisingly. *Not really so surprising. Your cat came to you easily, so I'm thinking she was there all along. She knew us for what we are.*

She moved to each of them and they all rubbed against her. Neal was the last and he laughed when he moved along her body with his. She asked him what the hell was so funny.

Jules is going to be so pissed at us. We've all marked you now. It was necessary, but usually we ask for permission first. This is going to be so epic. I cannot wait to see what he does. She stared at him. He couldn't be serious. She looked at Bronwyn while the others looked at the house in front of them for a way in.

It's to relieve the tension and to have some fun with each other. They do stupid childish shit like that all the time. Neal and Alistair used to hug me just to piss Ryland off. Of course, the benefit to us is they feel the need to mark us again. It's…amazing.

It was nearing midnight when they shifted and dressed. Ryland said he would be point, but she told him she was. He argued with her for a few minutes until she took him down with a kick to the ankles.

"I'm better prepared to be point man. You're all big and nasty when it comes to being the big cheese, but this I know." He nodded but she could see he wasn't happy. "I promise next time we have to go into a vampire's lair you can be point man. Deal?"

"You don't have to be so sarcastic all the time. A simple 'I know more than you on this' would have sufficed." She cocked a brow at him and he laughed. "Okay, no it wouldn't have, but you're going to pay for knocking your big, bad, nasty male on his ass."

She could live with that so long as there was a next time. The door was unlocked when they entered, and she moved through it slowly. Memories of the last time she'd done this with someone made her take a deep breath, then another before she entered. Neal and Brock were going around to the back, Em and Ally were going to the one of the basement doors, and Bronwyn and Rayne the other. They had everything covered, she hoped.

The house was dark when she entered first. A trick that Mason had taught her was to find a light switch and turn it on. It would help her and surprise the person who preferred the darkness. He'd been talking about a different kind of perp than she was currently looking for, but a perp was a perp, she supposed. The switch was right where she'd thought it to be, and she flipped it on. The entire entrance hall came to life with light.

Ryland came in next, with Alistair and Brock right behind him. Keith went to the right and Alistair to the left. She had them turn on lights in every room. When she and

Ryland started forward, he went to the stairs and she stopped him.

"She won't be in a bedroom, and she certainly won't have Jules in one either. Or she'd better fucking not have him in a bedroom. They'll be in a lair in the basement." He nodded and followed her. She was glad now that she'd talked to Peter before they left. She would have gone up, too.

There were two doors. She wasn't sure which to open and was just turning to Ryland when one of them opened and a…thing jumped out at her. She leapt back, but not quick enough to miss the claw that raked across her cheek. An inch lower and she would have lost her head. Taking the pencil out that she had in her hair to hold it back, she stabbed him in the back when he went for Ryland. He looked at her when the vampire disappeared.

"Nice trick. I'll have to remember to carry pencils around just to keep me from being attacked." She smiled and helped him up. "You're already healed. You must have some amazing powers locked away."

The scream from below them had them both tense up. Ryland called for Alistair and Brock and had them come to them. All three of them shifted, and she opened the door and led the way down. She knew the moment they passed through the door at the bottom that Jules was hurt, and hurt badly.

"How nice of you to show up. And, look, you brought me some kitties. They are lovely, aren't they? They will make a nice rug for my front parlor."

Lenny looked at her mother for the first time. "You're not going to get the chance to touch any of us, Divinity, or Naomi, or whatever fucking name you're calling yourself now. I have plans to kill you." Her mother laughed, and

Lenny felt her hair dance along her skin. When she walked to a wall covered in silk, Lenny nearly cried out when she saw Jules hanging there. He had a knife sticking out of his chest and blood on his face.

"I think these cats will do anything for their brother, including bringing me my daughter." Lenny didn't look at Ryland, but she wanted to ask him if she'd heard her correctly when someone touched her mind. She felt relief that it was Jules, but he sounded very weak.

She doesn't know. Don't tell her, but she has no idea even what your name is. Jules lifted his head slightly, and she saw that he'd been bitten, too. *I love you. Will you please make it so that we can get the hell out of here? I've got a major headache and my chest hurts.*

Tears blinded her for several seconds, and she looked back at her mother. She thought she'd won and that any minute now someone was just going to bring a daughter to her and she'd simply kill her.

"You should know that what we're doing is decreed by the Holder of the Realm. And as such, we are hereby ordered to mandate you to them and—"

Her mother came at her, and before she could raise her gun to fire at her, the gun was flying across the room. There was no way she could try and reach it. Then she heard a command to shift barked in her mind, and she was rolling on four feet rather than two. Turning to see her mother, she leapt at her as she stood there staring.

Claws tore at her flesh as she tangled with the pissed off vampire. Every time Lenny thought she had her, she'd snap her teeth into her and Lenny would move to get them out of her. When her mother clawed at her face, Lenny bit her hand off and spit it away, and was glad to see her mother screaming for a change. Taking advantage of her distraction, she clamped her mouth over her throat and bit down hard. All movement from her mother stopped.

"One minute, Lenny. Can you hold her?" She blinked at Brock, who stood over her as a man. "Viktor said to tell you not to kill her but to wait for the time."

"No." Brock looked at her mother when she spoke. "No. Must kill daughter now. Not be human."

"I'm sorry," Brock said with a smile. "I guess we should tell you who we all are. I'm Brock Golden, and that man over there helping my brother down from the wall is Ryland. Jules is the one you tried to kill. And that will go badly for you if you are brought to trial. And this lovely white royal is Lenore, Lenny to her friends. And she's also your daughter."

Lenny felt a sudden and profound pain run though her body and knew that her mother had clawed at her chest. She was off her mark if she'd been aiming for her heart. She had only seconds to move off the woman before the pain had her howling and snapping at her. Her cat stretched out and Lenny felt dizziness swamp her as every nerve ending in her body came to life with the pain. She felt hands on her, but it was too much and she whimpered. Then, as suddenly as it started, it stopped.

"Here you are, my dear." A blanket was tossed over her. "If you would be so kind as to shift to human, I should like a few words with you."

When she closed her eyes as a cat, she saw herself standing there as the cat had been. Her human self waved at her and started walking forward. When the cat moved to replace her, Lenny opened her eyes and looked up at Viktor.

"You'll need to attend to Jules. He is dying." She stood, quickly pulling the blanket around her as she went. "You'll need to save him with your new powers. You'll know what to do."

But she didn't. She had no idea what to do. "Tell me, damn it. I want you to tell me how to save the only person I've ever really loved."

"Lenny?" She looked down at Jules. "Kiss me, love. It'll be all right if you just kiss me. I love you."

She was crying so hard that she could see her tears as they fell on his face. She touched her lips to his and felt his coldness. Her heart broke because she knew she was losing him.

"Please don't die on me. You promised me you'd chase me in the woods and take me to the ground. You can't leave me, Jules. Please don't leave me." She kissed him again and held him to her. She looked up at Ryland, who took his brother's hand. "I don't know what to do. I don't know how to save him."

The scream behind her had her turn and she looked at her mother, who looked to be writhing in pain. At the same time a clock in the house somewhere chimed out the midnight hour. As she watched, Naomi seemed to age considerably. Gone was the twenty-something-year-old woman, and a dried-out, wrinkled one lay in her place. More and more changes took place as she got smaller and less human-like. Then she seemed to shrivel up and lay in dust.

Lenny looked at Viktor as he stood over her. "She became human. Now, my dear, it is your and your mate's turn. You will feel it soon."

Lenny looked at Jules when he stiffened. His body was glowing. When she put her hand over his chest wound, her fingers burned and she could feel something pour from her to him. When he opened his eyes and looked up at her, she felt as if a great burden was lifted from her.

He lifted his hand and touched her face. "Hello there, love. I've missed you. Are you having a nice birthday so far?"

She laughed at him. "Not so much, but it's getting better since you woke up. Do you have nothing better to do than to lay about this house while I worry? You should have more respect for me. I'm royalty."

He closed his eyes, and she felt her body relax. Brock and Alistair picked him up and were taking him out to the car that had been brought to them by Sandra. Just as Lenny stood up, she swayed just a little and felt the room tumble around her. Things were circling around so quickly that she had to drop to her knees.

"Look at me." She shook her head at Ryland as she felt so sick. "Damn it, look at me. I need to see if you're going to be all right."

"I'm fucking not all right, you moron. I'm going to be sick." She leaned over and puked up everything on her belly. Then she lay down. "Ryland, just shoot me. Please?"

"I'm not shooting you. Come on. You have to get up." He lifted her up, and she felt her knees give when he tried to stand her on her feet. "You have to move around, Viktor said. He said that you can't sleep yet."

"Tell Viktor that he needs to be shot, too." She was suddenly giddy. "I feel weirdly drunk. Are I drunk with you too?"

He growled at her and she laughed again. When he started cursing at her, she laughed harder. She had no idea why she thought he was so funny, when normally he was so stiff and bossy she didn't care for him.

Ryland was dragging her more than she was walking because she simply couldn't get her mind to make her feet work. When she put one foot forward like she wanted, she grinned at him. He glared back.

"You're drunk on power." She nodded and grinned bigger. "What I wouldn't do to have a camera right now. You're sloshed."

"I feel really spectacular, thanks. My whole body is humming." She looked around. "I should find Jules. I could hum all over him. You think he'd like that?"

"I have no clue. Will you please pay attention to what you're doing?" She fell against him, on purpose this time, thinking she would mark him. She had no idea if it worked that way, but it would be fur…fun if it did.

When she stepped out into the night, she looked up to the moon and nearly tumbled backwards. Ryland cursed again, but she was feeling better and pulled away. He was never more than a few steps behind her. She could feel herself getting stronger, but exhaustion was pulling hard at her. When she went to her knees this time, he wasn't going to be able to wake her, she knew. Whatever had needed to be done to her was complete, and she needed to sleep.

Lenny smiled when she heard him this time. Ryland was threatening her with all sorts of bodily harm. Closing her eyes, she was just glad to know that he'd get the opportunity to do so. Sleep took her.

Chapter 15

Jules snuggled into the warmth. He knew it was Lenny and decided that he was never moving from this position. He had all he needed right here. When she moaned, he opened one eye to look at her and noticed the difference in her immediately.

"Happy birthday." She opened her eyes and looked at him. "It is still your birthday, right? I mean, we didn't sleep it away, did we?"

She rolled over to him and he pulled her body to his. She licked along his throat and he felt his cock jerk to attention. When he felt her hand curl around his cock, he moaned and rocked into her.

"I don't really care, do you?" He shook his head as she rolled him to his back. "I was thinking that you can give me this for my birthday. Your body, I mean."

"It's yours." She sat up over him, and he groaned. "We really should be naked for this. I mean, if you want my body, I shouldn't be hiding any of it from you."

She put her hands in the ties of his pants and grinned at him. She had on the shirt to the pants he had on, and if he didn't miss his guess, he'd say she was naked beneath it. When he ran his hands up her hips, he found he was right. He took the tails of the shirt and ripped it open.

As the buttons scattered around the room, he leaned up and took her nipple into his mouth. It hardened more as he suckled at it, and he pinched the other one to make sure it didn't feel like he was ignoring it. When her fingers cupped the back of his head, he looked up at her.

"I want to be inside of you. If you want slow and easy later, I can do that, but you smell of other cats, and I need to claim you." She rocked over his cock, and he rolled her to her back. "Now, baby, I need you right now."

She tore his pants off from the back, and he lifted his body up just enough that she could pull them free of him. When he settled back between her legs, she wrapped them around him as soon as he entered her.

"Please, Jules, more. I need more of you." He moved his hands up her back and to her shoulders and grabbed her tightly in his hands. He held her still as he punched hard into her, and moaned when she cried out. "More. More now."

He slammed into her over and over as she cried out. When he felt his balls tighten and fill and his climax run along his spine, he licked at her shoulder. She tilted her head back, and he nipped none too gently at her throat. Her strangled "bite me" had his cat snarl at him to finish her, and he sank his canines deep.

Her scream made his cock thicken in her. When she leaned up and bit his shoulder, his balls felt like they were going to explode. As soon as she moaned, he jerked hard and felt her mark him, and knew it was going to scar, just like the kind of wound a male did to a female when he claimed her. His body detonated inside of her as he came, pounding in her as he filled her with his seed. It was all he could do not to drop right on her, and in the end that's just what he did. Christ, she was going to make him old before his time.

When she rolled him to his back, Jules sat up and took her nipple. She rode him as he suckled at each breast until he felt her tighten again. When she came again, screaming out his name, he held her tightly to him as his own climax, smaller but no less satisfying, roared from him. When he fell forward again and took them both to the bed, he held her as she started to relax over him.

He looked at the canopy over the bed as he held her. Looking around, he could see old furniture that had been well cared for, drapes that were very beautiful, and he would bet very old as well. There was a fireplace between the two large covered windows that he would bet were floor to ceiling. When he looked up again, this time at the ceiling, he saw punched tin in a design that looked like hearts and flowers. It, too, was well cared for. Looking to the other side of the room, he could see a grouping of chairs made of the same material as the drapes and another fireplace. Bookshelves lined another fireplace and this one was lit. He looked at Lenny when she lifted her head.

"Where are we?" She shrugged and looked around, too. He sat up when she rolled to her back and got a good look at the room. "This isn't my apartment, and I'm pretty sure that none of my brothers have a room like this. And if there was a hotel that looked like this, I'd buy it. There would be a fortune in owning one like this. Look at this place."

He found a suitcase open on a chest and pulled out a pair of pants. There were clothes in it for Lenny as well, and he handed her one of the tee-shirts and jeans. He supposed he should have given her the panties and bra as well, but thought it would be fun if she went commando, too. They both went to the bathroom, and she whistled.

"Christ, look at this. Gold spigots, nice tile, and a shower built for seven hundred." He pulled her into his arms and nipped at her neck. "Are you thinking what I'm thinking?"

He kissed her. "If you're thinking we should take a shower, then hell yeah. I'm thinking after the bout of fantastic sex we just had, we could use a nice scrubbing."

She reached in and turned on the water, but before they could strip down again, someone knocked on the door. He thought maybe they should ignore it, but as they had no idea whose house this was, they should probably be nice. But damn, he wanted her again.

The door opened as they were exiting the bathroom, and a staunch looking man in a suit bowed. Jules looked at Lenny when she giggled. The man held out a small tray with an envelope on it.

"My lord, my lady, there are several people awaiting your arrival in the drawing room. They have requested me to come and...fetch you." He held out the note. "The elder Golden has requested you have this."

"Elder? My mom?" The man nodded. "If you want to live for a while longer, buddy, I'd refrain from calling her elder."

He read the note, then handed it to Lenny, who looked at the man hard. "It says here we're to meet with attorneys for the estate of Divinity. What does this mean?"

"I'm sorry, my lady. I have not been made aware of anything other than three days ago the two of you were brought to this suite and I was told to care for you. I have done so to the best of our abilities." He looked nervous and Jules almost felt sorry for him. "There is a man downstairs that I have seen before when the other mistress was in a foul mood. But there...I do believe that he is somewhat of an authority figure."

"Viktor Ravengric." The man nodded at him. "Okay. Can you tell them we'll be down soon?"

"Yes, sir." He started to leave the room but turned back, nervousness still on his face and in his stance. "Will you be requiring sustenance? We haven't had to...you are not vampires, are you, my lord?"

"No. We're tigers." The man didn't even blink, but he could see the relief on his face. "Yes, something to eat would be great. Sandwiches and whatever else you can find would be great."

Lenny nodded, too, and the man left. He looked at her and she sat down. She looked as confused as he felt. When he grabbed up a shirt to go with his pants, he handed her a bra and panties to go with the shirt and pants. Now that they had to meet with the authorities, both of them had to behave, he supposed.

"I think something is off about this." He laughed at her. "I mean, he called us 'lord' and 'lady.' What the fuck is up with that? Not to mention he didn't say we checked in to this place. He said we were brought here. And where is here?"

They moved into the hall and tried not to look like country bumpkins as they walked to the stairs. This was beyond a hotel and more like someone's house. There were things here that Jules had seen in fine galleries behind glass. He stopped to stare at a large vase sitting on a pedestal at the top of the stairs.

"It's mine." Lenny touched it softly. "I made this about five years ago for someone. I never knew who. You think we're staying here because he wants me to commission another piece for him?"

"Don't know, but some of this stuff is the real deal. No fakes. Whoever this guy is, I hope he has receipts for this crap." He laughed. She sounded like a true cop and him the artist. They held hands as they came into the entrance hall. Lenny stopped moving and looked at him.

"This is my mother's house." He looked around, having never seen the house when he'd been brought there. "You think they want to put me in jail for her dying?"

He didn't see how it was her fault, and they both went into the room that voices were coming from. Lenny launched into a tirade that had him laughing. His entire family was staring at her as if they'd never seen her before. He supposed they hadn't seen her like this.

She'd changed a lot. Her face and body were the same, but they were fuller, her skin softer, and her hair, fiery red before, now seemed to glow with it. And her eyes? Christ, they seemed to glow with a shade of green he'd never be able to duplicate in any medium. She was simply more than beautiful now; she was gorgeous. And the first person she just happened to see was Peter, and Jules almost felt sorry for him. Almost.

~~~

"I will not be responsible for her death. The bitch deserved to die, but I didn't kill her. When she became human, I guess her age caught up with her, but whatever the reason for her just shriveling up like an old apple, it had nothing to do with me. And absolutely nothing to do with Jules. So whatever burr you have up your ass about her being dead, take it to somebody who gives a shit, because I certainly do not." Lenny looked at Viktor when he clapped his hands and stood. "You are on my shit list, so if you value your balls I suggest girth up, because I'm gunning for you, too."

"You should know that these people are now beholden to you for the death of the shriveled up apple." Lenny flushed, having not noticed the others in the room until Viktor spoke. "And these people are the attorneys that your mother-in-law spoke to the two of you about when she sent the message up."

Ryland laughed, and she might have hit him if he hadn't been holding his little girl. Gabby crawled from his lap and made her way over to her and put her arms up. Without thinking, she reached down and picked the little girl up and held her. Gabby snuggled into her neck and sighed.

"Perhaps we should tell you why we're here." Lenny thought that was a good idea, too, and sat down when the man who'd spoken stood up. "This is the deed to the house, and we are not taking our usual cut from the accounts but giving it with the house as well as —"

"Deed to what house?" Alistair stood up and walked over. "I'm her attorney, and I work for the Realm, and as such, I'm going to be the one you deal with."

She started to tell Alistair that she was going to deal with his ass, but Gabby kissed her mouth just then. Bronwyn laughed from across the room. She just knew she'd put her up to it. While Alistair talked with the attorney, she looked around the room. She wondered why they were all there and why she and Jules were. Keith got up and handed her his little computer.

The screen had gone blank, but Gabby, even as little as she was, just reached down and opened it back up. She got off her lap and onto her uncle's when Jules came to sit next to her. Keith explained.

"This is the site that only a few of us can get to. It's the Realm's. See what this says? It talks about you and Jules and the rest of us helping the enforcers to take care of a nasty piece of work. They don't mention our names, but it's there." She looked up at him. "You're a hero to them, and they're trying to figure out how to repay you."

"For killing my mother." He shook his head, and Jules took the tablet and continued reading. "I don't understand. Who else did I help them with? And why, if you know, are we here and not...I don't know, at some sort of office?"

"When you took the roof off the mausoleum, you killed nine of the most notorious vampires we had on our books. Five of them were wanted in three different realms, and two more of them were wanted by others for murder of their makers. That is a crime that means certain death." The man sat down as Alistair and the other men moved away. "Do you know your new sister-in-law well?"

Lenny looked at Jules, then at the four women sitting talking quietly along with Sandra. She wondered if she'd ever feel that comfortable with them, and realized that she nearly did. She looked back at the man and nodded.

"Em had some very nasty family. One of them, the second oldest, had converted a great many people who were as bad as he. Winfred had decided that he was above the laws governing us, and had not given any of his children any training, only telling them to kill when they fed." She held Jules's hand when he curled his into hers. "There were five of his children, the last of them, inside that building. You also took out the others that have been mentioned, and two that were...they were responsible for the death of your friend and colleague, and your injuries. You helped us more than anyone will ever know."

"Why?" He looked at her oddly. "Why didn't you get up off your ass and take care of them yourself if you knew what they'd done to me and Mason? Or for that matter, if you knew about Em's brother's activities, why didn't you get out there and take care of his kids? You knew about them, didn't you?"

"It is not our place to kill, my dear. It's to hire others to—"

"You mean to hire hit-men. You're not much different than the people I just killed." He sputtered at her, and Jules squeezed her hand, but she was on a roll. "You sit up in your ivory tower and let things go for a long time before you get around to getting someone else to take them out. Then, when they do, you come and tell them what a wonderful job they did for you and pay them. You're a hit man. You can pretty it up anyway you want, but that's what you are."

Her cat stirred along her skin when the man stood up. When he took several steps back, she stood as well. He stared at her for several seconds before he smiled. She didn't like that smile any more than she did the man whose face it was on.

"Would you shift for us?" She shook her head. "I assure you no harm will come to you, but it would be very helpful to me if you did."

"Helpful how?"

Ryland stood up and walked to her. She wasn't sure if it was to protect her or to beat her ass. He looked thunderous.

"She isn't a trained animal." The man nodded at Ryland, then took another step or two back when the rest of the Goldens stood up and came to her. "She will not shift until you explain yourself. I'm male here, not you."

"I understand. I was…I saw her cat just now. She has great control over her for a newborn, do you not think so? But her color is…unusual, wouldn't you say?"

"Lenny, what's going on? How did these men see your cat?" She looked at Jules. "You shifted to save me."

She nodded at him, then looked at the man. "You know what color I am. So what? You think you can change that to suit you as well?"

"No, my lady, but if you are a white tiger, we will need to know. It will have to be marked in the books as such." The man looked at Ryland. "Is she a white tiger?"

"No. She's not a white tiger." Lenny waited for him to say more, but he simply crossed his arms over his chest. *Don't shift unless I tell you or they harm you. I don't trust these people any more than you do. And I didn't lie. According to legend you're not a white tiger to us, but a snow tiger. Big difference.*

Really? How is that, you moron? You don't think when he finds out you're lying to him he's going to be pissed? She felt his mental shrug and wanted to smack him. *I guess you're thinking I'll save your ass if he comes for you then. Don't count on it, big boy. I don't like you that much.*

Yes you do. He took a step forward, then stilled when Jules touched him. She watched the two men and knew that they were talking. When Jules looked at her, she knew that Ryland told him. Before he could say anything, Alistair stepped back to them.

"Boy, are you going to be thrilled with this shit." She took the file from him. "You are now richer than we are as a family. Congratulations, Lenny, you are a billionaire and a homeowner."

She sat down hard and looked at the file without opening it. Jules took it from her and as she stared at the floor, he flipped through the pages. When he took her hand, she felt him kiss the back of it, but was still reeling. She realized that Alistair was speaking to Jules.

"This house, along with all the contents, is hers. As are houses in Paris, Spain, and Germany. She has stock, a great deal of it, in seven of the ten most profitable companies on earth, as well as several bank accounts. The reward that was offered as the bounty on the men and women that were taken out is enormous, not to mention the jewels, paintings, and other items that are in the vault in the basement. Hell, the wine cellar alone, according to this paperwork, is worth a hundred times more than Neal's, and he's been collecting for years."

They talked, and she zoned out. She heard Ryland talking, as well as Brock. There were loud voices, but she wasn't really listening. All she could think about was that she had a great deal of money. She stood up and moved to the door and out of the room. If anyone said anything to her, she had no idea. She ended up in the kitchen, where there were several staff. They started to leave, but she asked them to stay.

"I'd like to…I just found out that this house is mine." The man from earlier nodded. "I'm sorry. Who are you?"

"I am…I am called Butler, my lady; this is Cook, and these ladies are called whatever you wish." She heard his hesitation there and wondered what her mother had called the three women. "Would you like something to eat?"

"I would, but I'd like to know your names, not what she called you. And I'm sure that it will take me a bit to remember them...." She looked at them. "Were you here of your own free will?"

"No, my lady, we were not." The butler glared at the older woman when she spoke, and she glared right back at him. "We've been told to stay on to see if you wanted us, too. We've not anywhere else to go, but we'd try."

Lenny sat down and nodded. "She didn't pay you, I take it. If you stay, I will. I don't know anything about a big house...hell, I know nothing of a little one either, but I won't treat you like she did. I'm not perfect and I have a foul mouth, but I won't hurt you."

They didn't say anything for several seconds while she sipped her glass of water. The cook sat down across from her. Then the others sat at the large table as well. He watched her and she let him. She knew he was a wolf.

"You'll not feed from us?" She shook her head no. "Then I'll be a real cook and not a man who disposes of the bodies when she gets finished with them? I'd like that very much, I think. To cook I mean."

"No. I don't...you'll have to tell me where the bodies are so that their families can have closure. And before you ask, no one will ever know where the information came from."

The butler refilled her glass just as Jules came into the room. He was offered a chair, and he sat next to her. Cook put out his hand and smiled at her.

"I am Cecil Pugh. This is Duane Andrews, your butler. The younger maids are Jillian and Bridgette, and this is Mrs. Lane. She runs the place, as does Duane. Welcome to what we called the Hell. But I'm sure you can think of a better name for this pile of bricks."

"I think I can. How about we call it Golden Abbey?"

Chapter 16

Jules wanted her. Not just now, but forever. He'd been walking with her and Duane for the past hour, just looking over the house and noting the improvements that it needed, when he'd had enough. Taking her hand into his, he cleared his throat.

"Duane, I'm sure you understand what needs to be done. Why don't you just do whatever it takes to get the house back up to par, and let us know of any costs over five grand? However, the roof needs repaired immediately, and I agree with whatever else you can think of." The man nodded, then smiled. The man got what he wanted him to do before Lenny did.

"How are we supposed to know what gets done or not?" Jules took her into what he thought was the room they'd been in earlier and was happy to see it was. It had been cleaned up, too. Too bad he was going to simply mess it up again.

"When it's no longer broken, he had it fixed." He pressed her against the door that he'd just closed and locked. "I don't really care about the house right now. I do care about you being naked and in that bed as soon as possible."

She cupped his ass and brought him closer to her. "I didn't think you'd ever get bored with this shit and simply toss Duane back to the kitchen."

"Why, you brat." He laughed. "I was bored to tears when he showed me that first bedroom and the next nine as well. How many bedrooms does this place have, anyway?" Not that he cared, but the taste of her throat was making him wild and he needed something to calm him. "I want you."

"I want you as well, but you made me a promise." He lifted his head and looked at her. "You said you'd chase me through the woods and take me there."

His body stiffened, and he felt his cat snarl at him. He wanted her, too. Pulling away from her body, he took off his shirt. Then the pants he had on. She watched him, panting.

"I want you to shift for me first. Then we're going to walk through the house so that the servants can get used to seeing us. I would hate to have one of them shoot us while we're playing in or out of the house." She nodded and pulled off her shirt and dropped it to the floor. Next came her bra, and it fell from her fingers to join his clothes.

"You do know that I'm white, right? I mean, no stripes at all. You think that will freak them out a little?" He didn't really care and told her. "I don't know what I look like either."

"You didn't see yourself?" She shook her head. "Why not? I remember going to the mirror to see me first thing."

"I had a mate to save." He flushed. "You're a great deal more important than what I look like as a cat. Ryland told me what I looked like."

He had told him as well. He'd said she was pretty. In fact, Ryland told him he'd been impressed with her, too. That her ability to shift without much in the way of training had impressed Keith when he'd told her how. Jules pulled off his pants and stood before her, naked. She leaned over to pull off her pants and shoes, and he nearly whimpered. She was glorious.

"Shift for me." She nodded and closed her eyes. He watched her as the cat took her. And his brother was almost right: she was impressive, but she was also the most beautiful creature he'd ever seen.

Her cat lay down and he moved toward her slowly. She wasn't used to him and he didn't want to startle her. When he was within a foot of her, she stood up and he knelt down to her. She was big for a female; as big as him when he was a tiger, he'd bet.

"You're lovelier than I've ever seen." He scratched her head when she lowered it to him. "Christ, I've never seen a full white tiger before, not even in captivity. I think Ryland was right in not telling the Realm what you were."

I'm a snow, he said. A snow tiger. He nodded at her. *Do you think you could shift now? I want to go out and play.*

He laughed. "Yes. But two things you'll have to remember while in the house. One, you're not going to have any traction like you would in the woods; and secondly—and this is important—you can't chase the help. If they run, you're going to want to run them down. But don't. It'll be hard enough getting anyone to work for us, but if you eat one of them, it will be impossible."

He opened the door and let his cat take him. He hoped someone in the kitchen would be there and they wouldn't mind opening the door for them, or he'd have to shift again to do so. Leaving the bedroom, he moved down the hall with her, encountering one of the maids. She looked at them and pressed herself against the wall, but she neither screamed nor ran. He would have to talk to everyone once they were better settled.

The kitchen was full of people. Duane and Cecil were there, along with several others that he'd not seen before. When one of the younger men started to dart out of the room, Duane barked an order for him to stay still.

"They are the mistress and master, you fool. Would you like to be served up on a platter for them? Stand still, all of you." Lenny moved toward Duane and rubbed her head on his leg. She marked him. When one of the others came toward her, she did the same to them. Jules sat back and watched. She was claiming them as her pack.

As Cecil moved slowly toward the door and opened it, Lenny went out first. As soon as she was in the grass, she started to roll around in it like a kitten would. Someone stepped up beside him and spoke. He glanced up at Mrs. Lane as they watched Lenny.

"She is a beauty, is she not, sire? So beautiful and child-like for something so large and deadly, I think." Jules stood up when Lenny took off to the woods. "I'll have a door put in for you, sire, if you wouldn't mind. And some clothes, if you'd like, put out in the outer building just beyond."

He looked up at her and nodded. When she smiled and went back into the house, he wished he'd remembered to mark her as well. They would be able to communicate on a limited level, but he could thank her. When the door closed behind her, he wondered what would happen with all of them now and turned when he heard Lenny roar. He knew she wasn't in trouble, but he took off after her anyway.

Mrs. Lane said to tell you that she will leave us clothes on the stoop and if we're a mind, she'd put us a nice chest out there and keep it stocked. She laughed. *I think I like her.*

I do as well. He leapt over a large log and saw a flash of white. She'd be easy to spot, he realized, even in the dark. When he saw her again to his left, he took off after her. Soon he was standing in the middle of a grove with no idea where she was. He lifted his head to sniff the air.

You're not finding me. He growled low, and she laughed at him. *Can it be that the great and powerful Jules has lost his mate?*

You have your scent everywhere and that of the people you touched in the house. Then it occurred to him. *You weren't just marking them; you were getting their scent on you so that I couldn't find you. You're going to pay for that.*

Keith told me that one. He said he does it when he wants to hide from you guys. I think it's great.

Jules was going to kill his brother the first chance he got. Then he smiled. No, he'd tell his mate that when he found her. He was going to tell her everything he knew about hiding. When he saw her dart past him again, he followed. She was proving to be hard to keep up with. When he found her near a tree, lying down, he moved up behind her and stood over her.

You're going to pay for teasing me and marking a bunch of men. She rubbed her head over his shoulder, and he licked her head. *I love you.*

And I love you, too. When he moved off her, she stood up as well and rubbed her body all along the left side, then up the right. He'd been right about her being as tall as him; she was only an inch or two shorter than him, but probably just as muscular. He purred when she moved back down his body again.

When her shoulder was near his head, he nipped at her. He wanted her. Badly. When she purred back at him, he bit her and watched as she tried her best to get away from him. He put his paw on her back and pushed her to the earthen floor. She didn't go down easy.

I want you, but I feel the need to fight you. He growled at her. *Jules, please tell me what to do.*

Lie down and put your lovely ass in the air for me. When she growled again, his cat snarled at her. She was pissing him off, and Jules thought she knew it. *He's going to bite you.*

I fucking hope he knows I have sharp teeth, too. Moving so that he was over her, he pressed her harder to the earth and felt her resistance like he knew his cat wanted. When he entered her, she snarled at him again, and he bit down on her shoulder hard.

She purred then. Surprisingly, his cat let her go and licked the wound at her shoulder. The blood stood out in stark contrast to her white fur, and Jules felt badly for it. When she moved her ass again, his cock jerked to attention as if to say, "Hello? Well?" He moved in and out of her slowly.

You're mine. He felt her purr. *All of you. And when you go into heat in a few months, I'm going to fuck you hard and spill my seed in you.*

Please. He moved his head along hers, and he felt her tighten around him. She was close to coming, and that surprised him. He'd thought that cats, female cats, didn't enjoy mating like humans. When she cried out, her sheath strangling his cock, he sank his teeth into her muscled shoulder and felt her come again.

Even as she tightened around him for the third time, making his cock hurt and moving difficult to do, he came.

Lifting his head from her shoulder, he roared out his release, knowing that anyone within a few miles would know and understand the sound. When she roared out as well, he bit her again just because he could.

He dropped over her, panting. He lifted off her only when she moved beneath him. When he rolled to his side, he shifted when she did. Lying down on his chest, he held her.

"I'm not sure what to do about all that's happened today." He ran his fingers up and down her back as she continued. "I've never been one for material things, and now I'm…well hell, Jules, that house is bigger than the block I lived on. And in answer to your earlier question, there are twenty-three bedrooms in the house, even if you don't count the ones in the lower levels. What did she need that many rooms for when she couldn't sleep in any of them?"

He told her he didn't know. "I'm sure we'll get used to it. If not, we'll get it fixed up and try to sell it. Though, I have to tell you, I doubt very much we'll have many buyers for a house that big."

"No kidding. Duane said that in addition to the bedrooms, there are ten full baths, a dining hall that will seat one hundred and fifty guests, a second kitchen to feed an army, and a pantry that will supply most grocery stores, though he did say they'd not had anything in it other than for their own meals since the place was built. I told him to stock it up well." She sat up over him, and his cock stretched a little. "But there is one advantage to having a house this big. We do have all those bedrooms to use."

He leaned up and took her nipple in his mouth as he moved her up to where she was over his cock. When he lifted her up, he took her mouth as he moved her over him. She took his cock in her hand, holding him as he lowered her over him. After she was seated, he helped her wrap her legs around him.

"This is the way I'd like to wake up with you every morning. Naked in either our bed or out here. But most assuredly, you wrapped around me." She rolled her hips, and he held her tightly to him. "That's it, baby. Ride me."

He held her, sampling her flesh as she moaned and purred at him. When she pressed him back to the grass, he let her, rolling her to her back once they were there. He was kissing her deeply before she could say a word to him, because if she turned him down, he was going to be hurting.

"Come, love. Come for me." She tightened her legs around him as he moved in and out of her. She was wet and tight, and he wanted to taste her in the worst possible way. When she lifted her body up just enough to brace her hands on his shoulders, he leaned up and took her breast in his mouth. She came screaming out his name when he lifted her ass and tilted her so that she was taking him deeper.

"Jules, come with me. Please, I need to feel you come now." She licked along his shoulder, and he did the same to her. When she sank her teeth into him, he felt the sharp prick of her teeth and came roaring against her as he, too, came. Christ, he was dizzy from it. He closed his eyes from it and felt his body relax. He was asleep in seconds.

~~~

She found him in the office. Lenny had been on the upper levels when Duane had called them on the phone. The flipping house was so large that she'd made the staff use phones to call them rather than trying to hunt them down. So far it had worked out well. Jules was talking on the house phone when she sat in the chair across from him. When he hung up, he looked at her.

"That was my agent. I have a month off before I have to get back to work again. I'm glad now that I'd made these arrangements before we moved in here. And the builders are starting work on my new studio tomorrow." She nodded. "Also, you should know that the pantry is filled and we won't have a problem like we did last night."

The staff had been very upset when Jules's family had shown up to help them move in. Duane had been mortified that there wasn't even a loaf of bread in the house, as the delivery people were set to show up in the morning. It turned out to be a large semi full of food, as he'd never ordered before for a master and mistress that ate food and went a tad overboard. But it had all fit.

They had ordered pizzas and beer and had invited the entire staff to eat with them. It had been a great deal of fun.

She realized that Jules wasn't speaking, and she flushed. "I just heard from your brother. The Realm wants to hire me to work with him and Em. They want me to be their onsite expert. What the hell do I know of paranormal murders and stuff?" She watched him reach behind him and take a book off the shelf and bring it to her. It was a thick book and she looked at the title. It said "The Goldens" in a beautiful script.

"It's from our family library. Mom brought it last night and said to give it to you. She said that a cat like you is mentioned in it. But it was in the early thirteenth century and you're the first in all that time to be a fully white cat." He opened it and showed her the handwritten pages. "It says that she was killed just after her first change. Probably when she was hunting, Mom thinks. You should read it and you'll be fine."

"You knew about this job offer?" He shook his head. "I don't know what to do. And thanks to your brother, I'm no longer a suspect in the death of Mason."

"I'm glad. Alistair said once he showed them the error of their ways, they straightened up pretty fast." She would just bet. Alistair wasn't a pushover, and she'd bet he was hell on wheels in the courtroom.

"I've gotten with your mom. She and your sisters are going to help me get the house in order. I'm not sure what that means, but I have a feeling it's going to mean some shopping." She shivered. "I'm not much of a shopper. And Rayne said she was taking me to her favorite shop to see what toys they have. I have a feeling it's not going to be anything we'd ever need for a kid."

He laughed. "No, I'm sure it's not. What else is bothering you? Something is. First of all, you're still sitting and not pacing like you do; secondly, you're much too quiet. What's going on?"

She did get up to pace and was glad when he didn't say anything. "I've been talking to the staff. They think we need to bring in at least a dozen more people to run this place. I can see their point, but I don't want to be responsible for hiring them. Or for that matter, firing them when they fuck up. Then there's the town nearby. Did you know that they are terrified of us? They think we're going to come into town nightly and murder them in their beds. And just so you know, they have reason to feel this way."

"We should have an open house." She turned to look at him. "Seriously, we need to get to know the people here, and they need to know we're not like your mother…like Naomi."

She'd asked everyone to call her that from now on. She didn't want to call her mother, because as far as she was concerned, she never was. And next week, the only woman she'd ever known as her mom was moving in; her grandma had decided to take them up on their offer of moving in with them.

"I'm so not planning that thing." He laughed and told her he'd call in a planner for her. "Also…you should know that I've been thinking about the money that we found. I'd like to do something for the staff that was here with Naomi. I'd like to figure out a way to repay the help that Naomi had before we got here."

They'd found three large stacks of money in the vault, along with the biggest selection of jewelry she'd never seen. And calling the thing a vault was like saying that a bank was a piggy bank. It was a large fifty-by-fifty-foot room with shelf after shelf of things spread out on them. And under those shelves were safes with loose gems, as well as bars of gold and silver. The last one had been filled with twenty-four million dollars in cash.

"Do something how?" She sat down again and tried to think of a way to tell him what she'd been thinking. "Because I was thinking that same thing. And I'd like to suggest we divide it equally between them. Of course, we'll more than likely lose a few of them, but I think they'd stay on until we find replacements. They're very loyal to you."

"They like you, too." She flushed when he smiled at her. "Well, they do. And that's what I was thinking, too. That we'd give it to them and tell them…I don't know everything to tell them, but tell them we appreciate them very much."

Jules nodded, and she walked around the huge desk and sat in his lap. He held her for a few minutes before he spoke, and she closed her eyes to the sound of his voice, but opened them quickly when he said something she was sure she'd not heard correctly.

"What do you mean your mother has our wedding party set up? When are we getting married?" He told her when. "Tomorrow morning? Are you fucking insane? I can't...can't marry you tomorrow. I have to... I have to...." She had no idea, but marriage wasn't on the list.

"She said if you didn't show up, she'd hunt you down. You're just lucky I talked her out of having it here. She would have had this place decorated by midnight or hell would have been paid."

He handed her a pretty blue box. "What's this? If it's a ring, I thought we decided that we'd just use one of the millions she had stocked up."

"I didn't agree to anything. I merely let you ramble on. I wanted you to have something from me, not from the bitch from hell." She grinned at him when he took the box from her. "You are never going to be easy, are you?"

"Nope. Now if you do this right, I might thank you properly later." She knew that even if he'd told her to wear the fucking ring, bitch, and walk away before she could answer, she'd thank him properly after she beat the shit out of him for not doing it her way. She loved this man.

About the Author

Kathi Barton, author of the bestselling series Force of Nature, lives in Nashport, Ohio with her husband Paul. In addition to writing full time Kathi likes to spend time with her eight grandkids, three children and three children-in-laws. She writes to relax and have fun.

Her muse, a cross between Jimmy Stewart and Hugh Jackman brings them to life for her readers in a way that has them coming back time and again for more. Her favorite genre is paranormal romance with a great deal of spice. You can visit Kathi on line and drop her an email if you'd like. She loves hearing from her fans. aaronskiss@gmail.com.

Follow Kathi on her blog:
http://kathisbartonauthor.blogspot.com/